House with
Two Doors

Bilingual Press/Editorial Bilingüe

General Editor
   Gary D. Keller

Managing Editor
   Karen S. Van Hooft

Associate Editors
   Karen M. Akins
   Barbara H. Firoozye

Assistant Editor
   Linda St. George Thurston

Editorial Board
   Juan Goytisolo
   Francisco Jiménez
   Eduardo Rivera
   Mario Vargas Llosa

Address:
Bilingual Review/Press
Hispanic Research Center
Arizona State University
P.O. Box 872702
Tempe, Arizona 85287-2702
(602) 965-3867

House With Two Doors

Ricardo Pimentel

Bilingual Press/Editorial Bilingüe
TEMPE, ARIZONA

ISBN 0-927534-67-3

Library of Congress Cataloging-in-Publication Data

Pimentel, Ricardo.
    House with two doors / Ricardo Pimentel.
        p.   cm.
    ISBN 0-927534-67-3 (alk. paper)
    1. Mexican American families—California—San Bernardino—Fiction.
I. Title.
PS3566.I5145H68   1997
813' .54—dc21   97-9912
                                                          CIP

PRINTED IN THE UNITED STATES OF AMERICA

Cover design by John Wincek, Aerocraft Charter Art Service
Cover photos courtesy of Daniel S. and Eleanor M. Amparan and
      Theresa Armendarez
Author photo, page 169, by Laura Pimentel

Contents

Casa con dos puertas mala es de guardar
(A house with two doors is hard to defend)
—title of a 17th-century play by
Pedro Calderón de la Barca

October 3, 1967:
The Orange Show

Flashing lights, hawking carnies, the hearty laugh of a bearded fat woman beckoned passersby into the fun house. Screams wafted from the twirling, plunging, vertigo-inducing rides.

It was the annual San Bernardino Orange Show, and Gabby Rivera, Louie Maldonado, and Chuchi were drunk on atmosphere. Past the fun house and the twirl-a-whirls, the three strutted, a hand in one pocket, the other arm hanging free, a shoulder dipping, the upper torso bobbing and weaving side to side. The walk said, "No me chingas"—don't mess with me.

Elsewhere in the midway, youths more versed in the strut wore jackets over starched white T-shirts, above neatly creased brown or black slacks.

Gabby, Chuchi, and Louie had the swagger but didn't have the colors, the brightly decorated jackets that indicated gang membership.

A walk through the midway at the Orange Show was a perilous but mandatory gauntlet for the west side's macho adolescents—a rite of passage for those who wore colors and a pain-in-the-culo for la chota, the cops.

"Ay, qué chichona. Look at the chi-chis on that one," said Chuchi, Gabby's pachuco friend. Chuchi nodded toward a Mexican teenage girl with big hair. "Let's not go on any rides. She'll give us one," he said, laughing what he thought was a lusty laugh, lost instantly in the midway clamor.

Chuchi was imposing: short, stocky, and thick-chested. A tough street youth, he was very much unlike his two younger friends, but the three had been carnales ever since he had unsuccessfully tried to extort lunch money from Gabby years before. Gabby had offered to share his chorizo burrito instead.

Chuchi was Gabby's connection to the streets and Gabby was Chuchi's only link to stability. Both Gabby and Louie were, in gang lingo, "civilians"—not even wannabes. Chuchi knew, however, that he was fated to wear Lords' colors, and tonight he wanted to prove himself worthy.

The three were cruising. Not actually looking for trouble, but not likely to be very surprised if they found any. The midway was packed. La chota—always the last to know in San Bernardino—had no inkling of trouble brewing. Tonight, the feuding Lords and Gents had, by invisible telegraph, declared a truce, which was very bad news for chucos from the rival barrios of outlying Colton and Fontana.

Word spread quickly. Smart Colton and Fontana youth might choose to stay away, but in the strict macho code enforced in the area's barrios, to stay away would have been akin to letting a white boy steal your girlfriend.

"Hey, ése, what you lookin at?"

Gabby watched as the chief Lord, Joey Gallegos, hurled the challenge. The Colton youth stopped and, in the traditional counter-challenge, leaned back, shot his chin upward, and dropped his palms outward at his side as if to say, "What's your problem, cabrón?"

The midway lights still flashed. The aroma of sizzling corn-dog batter still wafted through the air. The bearded fat woman still beckoned. The rides still twirled. Gabby noticed none of it.

"Chuchi, let's go," said Louie, a big kid but at heart a peaceful one.

"Ése, where's your huevos?" Chuchi retorted.

The posturing had to be done in style. One couldn't just start throwing chingazos. First the ritual hurling of epithets and threats and the beating of breasts for the benefit of rucas and apprentice youth. It was Gallegos's turn.

Joey strutted up to the Colton teen, Flaco, a sallow-cheeked rail of a youth whose head was still tilted back and whose dark eyes simmered as he waited for the next step in the minuet.

"Vato, you're in Verdugo now. You don't show your colors here and expect to leave with them," said Joey, looking at the homeboys who were backing him up.

"Do you always need that backup pinchi. Or are you just lonely?" mocked Flaco, buoyed by his own homeboys.

Gabby was enthralled. Louie wanted a corn dog. Chuchi was impatient.

"Sheeee-it," said Chuchi.

The rival youths spread out, each choosing and sizing up likely opponents. Chuchi chose Flaco, who had already been chosen by Joey.

Chuchi stepped into the narrowing gap between the two, his head reaching only to Flaco's chin.

Flaco looked down into the smoldering brown eyes and made a mistake. He laughed. "Your chamacos do your fighting for you?" he said, sneering at Joey.

"This chamaco's going to kick your ass," said Chuchi, his left hand shooting up to grasp Flaco's throat, the other grabbing his crotch. He lifted the bug-eyed Flaco a couple of feet off the ground and threw him down then began kicking him with his shiny, black pointed shoes.

Gabby and Louie—they'd practiced the move in the half expectation, more like fantasy, of just such a gang-bang—positioned themselves back to back. They girded for the attackers. None came. The gang members were only interested in those wearing colors, the real players, but they were also very interested in Chuchi.

Gabby saw that Flaco's homeboys were converging on

Chuchi, who was swinging and kicking wildly, connecting every once in a while.

Gabby plunged into the fight. He wanted to pull Chuchi away and make him run. Chuchi was overmatched. Gabby's right eye intercepted a punch intended for Chuchi. He went down, but got up quickly. He made another grab for Chuchi, whose T-shirt was now in shreds and whose left hand was clutching a Colton jacket.

Into the melee came the chota blue suits. Heavily outnumbered, they pushed ahead, swinging the path clear with clubs and blowing whistles.

A blue suit charged toward Chuchi and Gabby. Chuchi didn't pay attention where his swings were landing. A crashing blow on the chest winded the cop. He fell on his butt.

"Chuchi, let's go," urged Gabby.

Chuchi's eyes cleared. With Gabby on one arm and Louie on the other, the three tried to force their way through. No way.

A hand landed on Gabby's shoulder. Bert, Gabby's older brother, jumped into the screaming crowd. Bert's friends followed. They carried Gabby, Chuchi, and Louie clear of the fighting, and then they all ran past the fun house, through the gaps between the corn-dog wagons, toward the Catholic War Veteran beer garden and taco stand, where the adults from Gabby's 14th-Street barrio were gathered for volunteer work. The mothers "volunteered" to make the tacos and the fathers volunteered to pour and drink the beer.

"What the fuck you think you doin?" yelled Bert, slapping Gabby on the back of the head.

"Don't tell Pop and Mamá. Please Bert," Gabby pleaded.

"It wasn't his fault, Bert," said Chuchi, trying on the Colton leader's jacket. The sleeves were a bit long, but they could be rolled up; he would wear the jacket after he had torn off the colors on the back.

Bert ignored him. "I won't have to tell. How are you going to explain that," he said, poking his finger into the mass below Gabby's eye. It was turning purple.

Gabby winced, shut his eyes, and knew, for a certainty, that tonight he was going to die. He could hear himself pleading, "No, Pop, no, Pop," as the belt came off slowly, loop by loop.

At seventeen Bert was not just bigger but calmer and more experienced. "Listen, ése, you're just going to have to face the music."

Bert sent Louie and Chuchi away and accompanied Gabby the rest of the way to the beer garden.

Fidel Rivera was telling his buddies for the millionth time how he won the Bronze Star in Korea. How he—a green infantryman, recently drafted—had been retreating from the hordes that poured over the Yalu to erase what gains MacArthur had made after Inchon. How he, a Negro cook pressed into duty, and other "fresh" troops were chosen for rear-guard duty while the seasoned veterans ran all the way back to Seoul. While weary but polite eyes glazed over, he told of that last-ditch stand to buy some time for the retreating troops, of the flying bullets and shrapnel that depleted the ranks until Fidel and the cook-turned-infantryman were the only ones left able to shoot.

"There we were, me and that negrito cook," Fidel was saying.

It was lucky for Gabby that Fidel was reliving his heroics; he was feeling expansive after many beers.

Gabby tried to sneak past, but Fidel grabbed him to give him a hug and a couple more dollars if he needed it.

"What's the matter, mijo? Look at me," he said as Gabby turned the right side of his face away from his father.

"What the hell happened? Bert, come here. Did you do this?" Bert stiffened.

"No, Pop," Gabby said quickly. "There was a fight in the

midway. They jumped Chuchi, and I couldn't just stand there and let him get beat up."

Fidel's eyes narrowed at Bert, "And where were you? You're supposed to be watching the chamaco. You were with that damn car again."

Bert stiffened. The time and money he spent on his '58 Chevy were a fertile source of family argument. Bert was a Chancellor, a member of a low-riding, shiny-auto car club.

"But Pop, Bert pulled us out of there after the cops came with their clubs," Gabby said, glancing at Bert, who relaxed.

Gabby looked expectantly at his father. Silence. The brow unfurrowed and the eyes crinkled in a smile as Fidel vainly tried to hide his pride. Hugging Gabby, he said boozily, "Go show your mother what a baboso you are." But he was smiling.

Gabby went to the kitchen to show Soledad. "Dios mío, ¿qué pasó?" she said as she smeared Rex lard on the lump below his eye and chided Gabby for hanging out with his "pachuco, malcriado friends."

Fidel motioned Bert closer, "Want a beer?"

* * *

Leaning up against the building housing the flower show, Chuchi admired his hard-won jacket. Louie had left to find his parents.

Absorbed in trying to figure out how he would get the colors off the back of the jacket, he didn't notice as the group of Lords surrounded him.

Joey Gallegos and the others stared at Chuchi for several long minutes.

"You got something that belongs to me," Joey said.

"What? You mean the jacket? Chale," Chuchi replied. "No way. I worked hard for it."

Joey continued to stare at the short, stocky youth, deliberating his next move. There would be no glory if he had to fight the younger boy for the jacket. Besides, after watching what Chuchi had done to Flaco, Joey wasn't sure it would be all that easy. He was hoping his stare would intimidate Chuchi into relinquishing the jacket.

He knew Chuchi only vaguely; knew him to be one of the several younger toughs on 14th Street who sometimes tried to tag along with the older Lords. He knew Chuchi had much in common with the Lords. Chuchi didn't seem to attend school much and was a problem in the classroom when he did. He spent much of his time on the street, which he found much preferable to going home to a mother who drank too much and brought home too many sleepover "tíos."

Joey saw there was no surrender in Chuchi's eyes. He looked around at his carnales, who were tensely waiting to see if they would have to take the jacket from Chuchi.

Joey nodded, not taking his eyes from Chuchi's. "I guess you did earn that jacket."

The other Lords relaxed. "Hey, Joey, we gotta go. La chota's over there," one of the Lords said, pointing to an officer just emerging from the midway crowd.

"Let's go," said Joey, leading the Lords to the same fence they had jumped to get in.

Chuchi went with them.

October 10, 1967: Fidel

Fidel Rivera was the product of a mixed marriage.

His father drank beer. His mother didn't. His father fooled around. His mother didn't.

Fidel was nothing if not a traditionalist. He was a remote and proud autocrat who loved his family dearly but reveled in the perks of machismo.

Fidel drank Burgie beer when he wanted—not to excess but enough to make the point. He worked at Santa Fe just like his father, who was also named Fidel. And, though he loved his wife, he had other women, just like Fidel the First.

Lying with Dolores, his current interest, Fidel thought how different she was from Soledad. Soledad put her hands on Fidel only to rub Vicks on his chest during his periodic chest colds. Dolores was always touching or wanting to be touched.

"Ay, qué hombre," she said afterward, her hands running smoothly down his chest to his belly and beyond.

"Give it a rest, woman," Fidel murmured, pleased. Dolores understood that men need to feel they've satisfied a woman, even if they haven't. Usually she was satisfied.

Fidel loved his wife, but Soledad, by his lights, didn't give him what he needed. Unlike Dolores, Soledad was not a demonstrative woman. Her affection for him seemed limited to standing by the stove while he ate to provide a constant, warm supply of handmade tortillas. Early in their eighteen-year marriage Fidel gave up his own displays of affection. They were only shyly and hesitantly received and never reciprocated. Soledad had been a rookie at lovemaking and she had not gotten any better in the ensuing years.

Fidel was not foolhardy enough to believe he loved Dolores. That was too bad for Dolores. Fidel was one in a line of men who believed she was good enough to use but not to marry.

"When am I going to see you again, Papá?"—her pet name for Fidel.

Fidel pulled up his calzones, baggy white boxer shorts. Once a week is enough, he thought.

Dolores lay on the bed, the sheets pulled over her breasts and her long black hair cascading down the pillows. She looked at Fidel's broad back and the soft love handles just beginning to roll over the elastic on the calzones.

Not the best lover she had ever had. Sometimes he was a little too quick. But she liked the feel of his big, callused hands on her, and his eyes were about the kindest brown eyes she had ever seen. There were frequent gifts and even a little help now and then with grocery and rent money.

The good ones are always taken, she thought. They first met at El Chino, the cantina and restaurant on Fifth Street where she worked and where the day shift from the nearby Santa Fe rail yard congregated after work. Fidel and Dolores always met at the small house she rented by La Esperanza Market.

She kept her refrigerator full of Burgie. At first she resented never being able to go out together and rarely acknowledging one another at El Chino when he came in with the rest of his sweaty Santa Fe friends. But Dolores admitted a grudging respect for Fidel's insistence on discretion. She realized that it came from the same kindness and gruff gentleness that attracted her to him in the first place. He didn't say it—he never talked about his wife—but Dolores knew that he must love his wife.

Dolores had accepted things the way they were. Until lately.

"Papá, are you coming tomorrow?" she repeated.

"Not mañana, Dolores. It's Bert's birthday. I should be there."

Her forehead wrinkled and her long slender nose pinched a bit.

"What do you want me to do? Just forget he's my son?"

Dolores got out from under the sheets. At twenty-six her once firm nalgas—buttocks—were just beginning to droop, but it wouldn't be something Fidel could see. Her black hair hung down well below her waist. She put on her slip and walked out to the kitchen.

"I didn't say nothing," she said petulantly on her way to the refrigerator. "¿Cerveza?"

Fidel looked at the peach-colored walls. His eyes rested on a picture of La Virgen. She held a baby, wore a blue robe with stars on it, and stood on ground embedded with small sea shells. Some had been pulled off or had fallen off.

Fidel wondered, as he always wondered when he looked at La Virgen, whether he should be feeling guiltier than he actually felt, which was not very guilty at all.

La Virgen stared at him, asking much the same question. She and Fidel had something of a special relationship. When he shipped out to Korea, his mother gave him a medallion of La Virgen, which he kept on the same chain as his dog tags. When he was scared, which was often in Korea, his hand would creep to that medallion. He'd feel for it through his uniform, pressing hard against it until it bit into his chest, a reminder that he wasn't as alone as he felt.

The dog tags lay in a box with his medals and other military memorabilia. The medallion was on Dolores's nightstand. Fidel was never alone.

"No, I got to go."

Without looking, he knew that Dolores's forehead was wrinkled and that her nose was pinched. Fidel supposed he wasn't being fair to Dolores. She could do better. But, dammit, he needed her. She knew it.

10

When Fidel walked through the door once a week, she could see the need in his eyes. She could feel it as his arms held her close and his hands worked their way up and down her back. She loved how he held her. She could smell what he had for lunch in the bushy mustache that drooped below his lips. It usually smelled of the tacos—sometimes chorizo— that his fat wife put in his banged-up lunch box.

At least, Dolores imagined that Soledad was fat. Fat and short and probably evil tempered. It was easier if she imagined her that way. She would have been disappointed had she ever met sweet-faced Soledad.

Dolores would leave Fidel openings to tell of his wife's evil temper, how she misspent his hard-earned money on frivolous things and denied him his due in the bedroom, but Fidel never availed himself of the openings.

So, Dolores just imagined and filled Fidel's needs.

But today Dolores was feeling needs of her own. She needed to feel life inside her, to have a brood of little brown children underfoot. She never used birth control. To do so would have been a sin and unthinkable. She had fully expected she would be pregnant by now with Fidel's child. She didn't know of his vasectomy. Had she known, she probably would never have let him in her bed. In her eyes, a man who neutered himself was saying no woman was good enough to have his children. It was a license to screw indiscriminately.

Fidel just figured it was none of her business.

The vasectomy was Fidel's sin—to stop the miscarriages after Gabby's birth—but his wife, Soledad, carried it into the confessional with her. "Bless me, father, for I have sinned. My last confession was last week. I've laid with my husband, knowing we can't make babies."

Father O'Leary was always understanding. "It would be Christian, daughter, if you asked your husband to come in for confession."

While Father O'Leary never actually counseled Soledad to quit sleeping with her husband, he hinted broadly. He didn't realize, however, that Soledad was no more able to say no to her husband than the Father was able to say no to those bottles of wine every night.

Meanwhile, Dolores, the mistress, was hatching a scheme. "There's a dance in Colton this Saturday. I haven't been dancing since I met you," Dolores said, bringing the beer he said he didn't want into the bedroom while he dressed.

"So, go," answered Fidel, quietly.

She knew she was treading on thin ice and deliberated whether to proceed. "Papacito, don't be that way. I just want to be with you."

"You're with me now."

"I know. But I want others to see how proud I am to be with you," she said.

"If I know and you know, who else needs to know? Go to the dance if you want. Just don't expect me next week if you do."

Double standards—men's prerogatives and women's duties—were something else Dolores and Fidel never talked about.

Silence filled the peach-colored room. Ten minutes earlier it had been filled with the sound of heavy breathing, slapping flesh, rustling sheets, and creaking springs.

Dolores's eyes moistened. Fidel's clenched jaw started twitching.

"I see you maybe an hour or two every week. Fidel, I'm twenty-six years old. My sister is younger than me and already eight years married and with four girls. Do you think it's right that someone as full of love as me should be using it once a week? I'm only asking to go dancing, not to have your huevos in my hand every minute you're awake."

Fidel felt La Virgen on the wall listening closely. On his

chest, her medallion rose and fell to the deep thumping underneath.

"Do you think men who work at Santa Fe don't live in Colton? Do you think people in Colton don't know me?"

"And if they saw you, so what? Every cabrón over there steps out on his wife." She was angry now. "If I had a dollar for every man from Santa Fe who grabbed my ass, I'd be a rich woman."

Having an affair with a passionate woman has its risks. They are as passionate in their anger as they are in their loving.

"If what we have isn't good enough for you, maybe you should find a man who will jump every time you squeeze his bolas. Maybe he'll say 'I love you,' " Fidel squeaked in falsetto, his best imitation of a man without huevos, "every time you squeeze. And what he'll really be saying is that he don't have no balls."

"Who's the one with no balls? You won't even dance with me. I like what we have. I just want more of it," she said, softening. "What's this talk of bolas. All I'm saying is that I want to get dressed up, to walk into some place that has people in it with my arm in yours to show them I'm not just your once-a-week puta."

A long pause.

"Maybe I'll go with Henry. He asked me yesterday."

Henry was Henry Macías, thirty-five years old, unmarried and still living with his mother, Simona, across the street from Fidel. Simona was Fidel's aunt—his mother's sister—and Soledad's best friend and confidant. Cousin Henry worked in the same crew as Fidel, cleaning railroad cars and inspecting each car's air lines, brakes, and other features.

Make Henry an Anglo, put a pen holder in the pocket of his shirt, which was always buttoned to the top, and you'd have a nerd. As it was, the elastic band that held his black-rimmed glasses, his butter-ball roundness, and the fact that he had been in the Navy all spelled weenie.

He was the kind of guy that every mother wished for in a son-in-law and every Mexican father hoped his son would not degenerate into. Henry accompanied his mother to 7 A.M. Mass every Sunday at St. Anthony's, where he was an usher and had been an altar boy years before. Some said it looked like his mother still dressed him.

The prospect that he would lose Dolores to such a one was too much for Fidel. "You do want a man without huevos," he said, but Dolores knew she'd be dancing with Fidel in Colton on Saturday.

October 11, 1967: Soledad

The kids were in school and Fidel was at work. She'd washed the dishes and a pile of clothes needed to be mended in the back room, where the old treadle sewing machine waited.

Soledad sat sipping her coffee at the Formica kitchen table. She stared alternately out the window and at the rows of pictures hanging in the hallway. There were fading photos of fathers and mothers, who were now all dead. There was a photo of Fidel in Army uniform, standing solemnly next to a smiling Soledad in her white wedding dress. There were baby photos of Gabby and Bert and a recent one of Bert with his '58 Chevy Impala. In his Chancellor's jacket, he stood proudly next to the metal-flake orange car that he had bought from earnings as a box boy at Stater Brothers market. Gabby smiled in various school photos that Soledad knew were also in family members' wallets and on their walls.

"It's a good-looking family," Soledad said to Pedo, the dog sprawled on the kitchen floor. Pedo looked expectantly at Soledad. There was a dish of breakfast leavings he knew would soon be his.

Pedo, fart in Spanish, was theoretically Bert and Gabby's dog, but Fidel named him. Fidel always said there were two kinds of people in the world: those who thought farts were funny and those who didn't.

Soledad hadn't thought the name was very funny five years ago when Fidel brought the dog home. Pedo was a Shepherd-Collie mix. Fidel insisted he chose Pedo for his instinctive guard-dog qualities, but the boys knew Fidel chose him because he peed on his shoe on introduction and because he looked a bit different from the rest of the litter. A short, bushy, rabbitlike tail protruded from the dog's butt. Pedo was part bear, Fidel told the boys.

The name—and the dog—grew on Soledad. Now Pedo was probably more her dog than anybody's. In private, Pedo was Soledad's confidant. When folks were around, he was the nuisance chased out of the kitchen with a broom, berated for shedding too many hairs in the house and for carrying home late-night carcass snacks, undoubtedly pilfered from neighbors' garbage cans. Pedo played along.

"Fidel was with his whore last night," Soledad said.

Pedo's tongue plopped out and he wagged his butt. He didn't have enough tail to wag.

The night before, Fidel had come in late, as he often did. Soledad warmed up his dinner, served him, and opened a beer for him. Long ago she had given up asking where he had been.

"Out," was the standard reply. Or, if he was in a foul mood, "¿Qué te importa, vieja?" What's it to you.

She had made small talk. She told Fidel that they had purchased Bert a new jacket for his birthday, that she wanted him to talk to Gabby about his pachuco friend, Chuchi, and that his sister called to ask if Bert and Gabby could clear some brush from her back yard. Small talk to fill the air and stifle the words that needed saying.

Later, in bed, she imagined she could smell the other woman, and, for the millionth time, she went over her own shortcomings, the ones that obviously drove Fidel away. Fidel made love to her that night by rote. He must be feeling a little bit guilty, she hoped. Actually, he was feeling a bit proud that he could do it twice in a night.

Soledad poured more coffee. She swept the breakfast scraps into the pie plate that served as Pedo's bowl. She looked at the framed needlepoint on the blue kitchen wall: Home Sweet Home, it said. She went into the hallway and stood before the wedding picture.

"I don't look so different," she said. Pedo wasn't listening.

In 1949, the year she and Fidel were married, she was seventeen. A few months after the picture was taken, she was pregnant with Umberto, Bert. She had spoken very little English back then. Although she had been in the country for four years, there was little need to learn. You could work at the laundry and speak only Spanish, even to the owner. You could live in a little house behind an aunt's house with two sisters who also had slipped across the border and not have to speak English.

You could shop at La Esperanza or at any of the other stores along Mt. Vernon and never see an Anglo face. You wrote letters to your parents in Spanish, the same letters that contained the money sent to help sustain those remaining in Zacatecas. You could even watch Cantinflas and Antonio Aguilar at the Azteca Teatro, the Spanish-language movie theater.

Fidel spoke Spanish, but only after a fashion. His feelings would have been hurt had he known how Soledad's sisters teased her about the "pocho's" Spanish.

The boys—that's how she always referred to Bert and Gabby—understood only as much Spanish as they needed to know. In a standard conversation, their mother spoke to them in Spanish, but they replied in English. It drove Soledad batty.

Soledad's heavy accent was a constant source of amusement to Fidel and the boys. They seemed happiest when they were teasing one another or her. That took some getting used to. It was a Rivera trait.

Soledad's announcement that she was about to go "chopping" at the store always sent them rolling. They also got a kick when Soledad tried to master one phrase or another, such as when she told Bert he was "pooching" her leg after he tried to sell her some unbelievable tale. That one went down in Rivera lore.

"I know my hips are a little wider. But I don't weigh much more now," she said in Spanish, still looking at the wedding photo. A little gray was visible in her hair now. She had cut her hair short. That was probably the first mistake, she thought. Fidel had loved her long black hair. It had been a nuisance to her, however, so one of her sisters, who now worked in a beauty shop, had cut it for her.

With a sigh, she started toward the sewing room, where clothes waited to be mended in tidy piles by the sewing machine. She stopped suddenly, and Pedo bumped into the back of her legs, then went into the room and took his place next to the sewing machine. Pedo was bilingual even if the boys weren't and would keep Soledad company through the day's work.

But Soledad didn't go into the sewing room. She put on her baggy sweater with pockets full of used and unused tissues and headed for Tía Simona's house across the street. In her blue moods Soledad often went to see Simona, not to confide but to listen to the old woman's cheerful banter and self-deprecating humor. A hunched back—they later gave it the name osteoporosis—gave Tía Simona a lopsided look, which was emphasized by her use of a cane.

Simona's favorite topic was her son Henry. The boy needed a wife, she'd say. He had just been elected secretary-treasurer of the local chapter of the Catholic War Veterans. Father O'Leary had asked Henry to take charge of this year's Christmas festivities. Something was always happening in Henry's life. Everything, that is, except meeting good women, a fact that distressed Simona greatly.

Too bad all of Soledad's sisters were married. Now, that's the kind of wife Henry needed, a Mexican woman, Simona would say. Not one of those agabachadas—Anglicized Mexicans—who think more of their dresses and makeup than of their husbands and children.

Today Simona was distraught. Henry had asked a waitress at El Chino to a dance. Simona didn't know this woman. Her name was Dolores. What kind of woman would be that old, unmarried and working, and who knows what else, around the rough Santa Fe crowd? It did not bode well.

"I'm to blame. I told Henry he wasn't going to meet women staying home with me every night," Simona complained. "I don't know this woman. Henry says she's from Tejas." Simona rolled her eyes. Texas conjured up all sorts of unpleasant thoughts. "Why isn't she with her family? Is she a good girl? Is she intact?" The old woman, also in a baggy sweater, dipped her pan dulce into her cinnamon-laced coffee. "I don't know. Maybe there are good girls in Tejas. But my sister's husband—not Fidel's papá—was from Tejas. Qué bruto. He hit her and ran around with other women."

Soledad winced but said nothing.

"Let's go to lunch today," Simona said suddenly.

Out to lunch? A novel concept, thought Soledad. Pedo would be disappointed. He usually shared Soledad's lunch. Well, he was getting fat anyway.

"Where to?" Soledad asked, dubious.

"Oh, I don't know. Maybe El Chino's. I hear the chile verde is good there." They both laughed.

"Maybe I'll even have a beer," said Soledad. Another daring act. Soledad rarely drank beer and never in public. What would Fidel think? No, she wouldn't have a beer.

The logistics of getting to El Chino were another matter. The Riveras had two cars, but one was Bert's and went with him to school. The other car, a four-year-old Impala station wagon, went with Fidel to work. It never occurred to either Fidel or Soledad that Soledad could drive Fidel to work and use the car rather than let it sit in a parking lot five days a week from 7 A.M. to 3 P.M. That would have impinged on

Fidel's mobility and male prerogative. That, at least, was the unspoken reason. That and the assumption that nothing was more important to Soledad than her household duties. A mobile woman is a woman with too much time on her hands.

Henry also took his car to work. Simona did not have a driver's license anyway and likely would have been dangerous on the road. In her present state she would have run over any woman who looked like she might be from Texas.

The pair decided on a combination of foot and bus. A ten-block or so walk to Mt. Vernon, a straight shot by bus to Fifth Street, and then another few blocks walking to the restaurant.

The trek would be harder on Soledad than Simona. Although she was sixty-eight years old, Simona spent much of her day walking around the neighborhood. She was the 14th-Street telegraph. She knew all the gossip: who was having a baby, who was drinking too much, whose sons were in jail or in the Army, who was getting married, and who was too soon pregnant.

She was something of an institution and, undeniably, the community's conscience. She presided at most rosaries when 14th Street lost someone. "Santa María, Madre de Dios . . ." she'd intone, while other sore-kneed grievants chimed in, casting chiding glances at giggling children who were not up to observing the solemnity of the moment.

Her cane was not so much to help her walk as to shake at any pachuco she came across. A scolding from La Señora was enough to send a Royal Lord slinking.

The neighborhood's generally fearless dogs gave her a wide berth, all except Pedo, who wagged his butt anytime he came across Simona. Week-old pan dulce went out on a plate on her back porch for Pedo. Woe to any neighborhood cat or dog caught in Pedo's dish. A caning by Simona usually followed.

Soledad was winded by the time they got to the Mt. Vernon

bus stop. Her only exercise these days was chasing Pedo out of the kitchen when she cooked supper, or playing catch with Gabby when Bert thought he was too old to play with his brother.

The walk had no visible effect on Simona. "Her dress will be tight around her cola. She'll probably have enough makeup on to paint my living room. Tejas," she spat, shaking her head.

Soledad pondered how best to tell Simona that beggars couldn't be choosers and that Henry was the romantic equivalent of a crippled blind man selling No. 2 pencils. "If Henry likes her, that's important," Soledad offered.

"If I like her, that's more important. Sometimes Henry doesn't know his own mind. Did you know he wanted to join the Marines? I told him the Navy was best. At least he learned a trade."

Henry was one of the few in the barrio to have not only finished high school but also to have taken some courses at two-year Valley College. He had been an all-purpose yeoman on an oiler in the Navy. He learned to type and how to keep books. He now did everyone's taxes in the neighborhood. He was especially adept at getting his clients tax refunds. Many a chain-link fence on 14th Street owed its existence to Henry Macías. Many a bright blue, green, yellow, or purple house on 14th Street could thank Henry for its gaudy hue.

If Simona had known about the brothels in the Philippines, Hong Kong, and Japan, her opinion of the Navy might have been a little different. Henry had gotten his share of the drip during his three-year hitch, but that managed to stay out of his letters.

"His own father," she made the sign of the cross, "wanted him to go into the Marines. It would make a man out of him, he said. I told him, what kind of man gets himself killed and causes his family grief?

"And women. He doesn't know what's good for him. He

would have married that Connie Jaramillo. She wanted to bad enough. Now we know why."

Connie had turned out to be pregnant. She had moved to Los Angeles and was not heard of again. Except by Simona, who heard from Connie's sister's husband's aunt that she now had two other children and was still unmarried, although she lived with the cabrón who got her pregnant in the first place while she dated Henry.

"Henry has had plenty of chances," Simona nodded her head knowingly.

Soledad coughed to keep from laughing.

The bus came. Soledad and Simona aboard, it went past Plaza Park with the bandstand in the middle, past the marquee at La Azteca, and past La Mitla restaurant. The Santa Fe smokestacks became visible, black smoke billowing from them. The women got off the bus.

"Her breasts are probably sticking out of her dress. Diseases. You can get diseases from Tejanas. Diseases that make men's pitos fall off." Simona laughed. She was getting into it now.

El Chino was so named because the proprietor was indeed Chinese. Lorenzo Lu was a fixture on Fifth Street. His Spanish was as fluent as his Cantonese. When he had opened the place thirty years before, he had to learn Spanish or go out of business. His original idea had been to serve the best in Chinese cuisine. Santa Fe tastes, he discovered, ran more to menudo, chorizo, and tacos.

Inside, red vinyl booths sat below murals of Aztec princes and their sacrificial beauties. Delicious smells of simmering and sizzling meat wafted from the kitchen. Tables in the middle of the floor took care of the lunch and dinner crowd. Through the arched doorway topped with toro horns was the bar, more tables, and a jukebox that dwelt heavily on rancheras and norteñas. After some beers, the gritos accompanied Javier Solís and others in musical laments about love, women, and treks north. "Aiiiiiyeee" to accordion and brass accompaniment.

Lu immediately noticed the two ladies come in. They were not his usual class of clientele but of the type he liked to encourage. Lately, the restaurant side had been harder to fill and the bar side too easily filled. That wouldn't have been so bad except that Mexicans drank mostly beer. Bars, Lu knew, make their best money off well drinks.

He'd make sure these customers left satisfied.

"Buenas tardes, señoras," he said, grabbing two menus, beating Dolores and the other girl to the front. They were good girls but sometimes too slow or too harried to extend the proper courtesies.

Soledad was taken aback. A golden-toothed smile and crinkled eyes beckoned the women. "This table by the window? Or would you like a booth," all in fluid Spanish.

Simona recovered first. "A booth, por favor."

Once Soledad and the old woman were seated, Lu told them that the lengua, beef tongue, was particularly fresh today. The cabeza, beef head, was always good, as were the nopales, cactus. The carnitas were good. Tortillas de harina or maíz were fresh daily from La Esperanza. Menudo was only on Sundays, but the cocido, a soup of large beef chunks, cabbage, potatoes, and carrots, was available. A waitress would soon wait on them, Lu said.

After he left, Simona and Soledad scanned the room. "Ay, Dios, I hope it's not the ugly India," Simona said, her eyes settling on a dark-skinned, rotund woman in a flowing skirt and peasant blouse. "I hope they wear name tags."

"She looks a little old for Henry," Soledad observed.

The dark-skinned waitress hurried into the bar, where a few drinkers were getting an early start and where she had just heard a glass shattering. Their eyes followed the woman. When their craned necks returned to normal position, they were startled by the other waitress already standing by the booth. She too had been watching the departing waitress.

She smiled, a beautiful smile that made her eyes sing and made her ordinary face something special. Soledad immediately envied her firm, pointed breasts, small waist, ample hips, and shapely legs.

"Tencha is always cleaning up after that bartender," the waitress said. By process of elimination, Simona determined that this was Diseased Dolores de Tejas.

This woman couldn't possibly be considering going to a dance with Henry, Soledad thought. Yes, she's a little old to be unmarried, but she could do better than Henry. As putas went, she looked pretty good.

How to begin, thought Simona, who immediately disapproved. Not even as pretty as Connie Jaramillo, and she probably spread her legs more often.

"Have you decided? I can come back a little later," Dolores said.

Simona decided an indirect approach was best. "Aren't you Domingo Cuervo's sister? We've met somewhere before," she said, stone-faced. "Maybe at Mass at St. Anthony's."

"No, señora. My name is Dolores and I've only been in San Bernardino for four years. All my familia is in San Angelo, Tejas. I go to Mass at Our Lady of Guadalupe," she lied. She didn't go to Mass except on Christmas and Easter.

Simona's back stiffened.

Dolores thought, what's wrong with Our Lady of Guadalupe?

"Disculpe," said Simona. "I thought you were someone else. I'm Simona Macías. Maybe you know my son, Henry. He comes in here often after work at Santa Fe. This is my friend Soledad Rivera."

Macías? Rivera? Rivera!! Dolores dropped her tray. It couldn't be, but she knew Henry and Fidel were neighbors as well as cousins.

Lu buried his face in his hands. What now?

"Sí, I know your son. One Coors after work and then straight home." Recovering quickly, she picked up the tray. "Have you decided?" she asked, casting nervous glances at Soledad. So this was Fidel's fat wife.

Soledad's suspicions were awakened. "Do you know my husband, Fidel Rivera? He also works at Santa Fe."

Dolores blanched. Soledad concluded that the waitress knew Fidel all too well. And she suspected also that, while Dolores might go dancing Saturday, Henry certainly wouldn't be dancing with her.

"I'll have a Burgie," Soledad said.

October 12, 1967: Bert

Bert was eighteen years old today. He had a good job, an a-toda-madre, bitchin' car, good looks, and true, por vida, love. His birthday party had been underway for a while, since before he got home from work at eight. Birthdays were impromptu affairs in the Rivera household, but there was one thing you could count on: lots of relatives dropping by with lots of food.

Uncle Chuy had long ago tapped the keg. After a few more beers he and the other uncles would be warbling, "Volver, volver." Fidel's and Soledad's brothers accounted for six uncles in the family. Husbands of sisters made seven more.

They weren't all at the party, yet it seemed like each had slapped Bert on the back, coaxed him into having a little beer—"I won't tell your pop, boy. Go ahead"—and imparted sage advice.

"Airborne. Special Services. If you've got to go, that's the way. You can get a three-year tour and teach those Viet Congas how we kick ass Verdugo style," said Chuy.

From Tío Rudy: "You're not messing around with that marijuana shit, are you, boy? You'd better not be. It'll break your mother's heart. I'll break your goddamn legs. Have some beer."

Cousins of various sizes and ages rampaged through the house and yard, ignoring admonishments to be still, behave, and watch younger siblings.

The women congregated in the kitchen, venturing out to the living room or backyard periodically to see who was misbehaving, who was drunk or getting there, and whether Chuy's new wife, Carmen, could be pried from her husband. The wives wanted to test her mettle in the kitchen.

Bert, in the clutches of Uncle Zeke, was glancing at Angie,

his girlfriend ever since he gave her his St. Christopher medal in seventh grade at Sturges Jr. High. He was hoping she would take a hint and rescue him from Uncle Zeke.

Zeke, Fidel's oldest brother, was the only independent businessman in the family. He had a barbershop on E Street and was also a part-time instructor at the barber college.

"Nobody gets haircuts anymore. Everybody has his hair *styled*." Zeke spit out the word. At the top of Zeke's shit list were long-haired hippies because they didn't want their hair cut or styled. Zeke's three boys stood out in any family gathering. Two wore white walls. The other had a flat-top with fenders, Zeke's idea of a style cut.

"There's no future in barbering, boy. Men are turning into girls. Your hair's kinda long. What are you going to do after graduation?"

This was a question Bert had pondered long and hard. Graduation from San Bernardino High School was a few months away. Mostly an indifferent student, except in auto shop, Bert knew he wasn't college bound. He knew he could cool his heels at Valley College and get a draft deferment, but he wouldn't be learning anything worth learning.

There were a couple of other possibilities. Mr. Burke at Stater's told him that he'd be willing to send him to cashier's school and take him on after graduation. Cashiers got paid well, about eight dollars an hour, enough to start a family on. Pop and a few of the uncles could grease the way for a job at Santa Fe. Angie's father owned an auto paint and body shop. He could start there, maybe get his own shop some day.

It seemed that almost everyone's pop on 14th Street and the west side worked as a laborer at Santa Fe Railroad or at the Kaiser Steel plant in nearby Fontana or as janitors for the city schools or as detailers at Berdoo's myriad paint and auto body shops.

None of that appealed to Bert.

Among Bert's friends, steeped in stories of their fathers' military exploits, the Army and Marines were the preferred choices; other young Chicanos veered toward the Air Force or Navy, hoping to learn electronics or some other useful trade.

The peer pressure was enormous. Some of his friends had already signed deferred enlistment papers. They'd be allowed to finish high school but would be in boot camp a few weeks afterward.

Elsewhere, antiwar feelings ran high. Flags and draft cards were being burned. LBJ was being hounded from office. Nationwide marches and rallies were being staged by those who, ironically, were not as likely as Bert and his buddies to ever be sent to Vietnam.

On the west side, however, military service was honorable, patriotic, and even quasi-mandatory.

The Mexican vets returning from World War I found that they were still expected to be San Bernardino's dishwashers, busboys, gardeners, and citrus pickers. But World War II and Korean War vets returned and found their lot improved. While few availed themselves of the GI bill's college benefits, many took advantage of the no-money-down, low-interest VA home loans. And they were grateful.

Predominantly blue-collar, the 14th-Street barrio was a haven for Mexican vets who returned from World War II and Korea with VA leverage to buy houses. Years later the same families were living in the same tract homes. With $100- or $150-a-month mortgage payments and friends and familia nearby, there was little reason to move away.

These vets firmly believed that on the beaches of Normandy, Okinawa, the Philippines, and other places they hadn't heard of before they began bleeding on them, they had served a noble cause. It was inconceivable to them that the president, even a non-Catholic president, would send young men to die in anything but a noble cause. Even

Soledad's brothers had been draftees in the Mexican Army before joining Soledad and her sisters in San Bernardino.

There was also a pragmatic reason for military service. Bert and his friends sensed that they were more likely to be drafted than their white classmates. They knew that tradition and family obligation would tie them to San Bernardino for the rest of their lives; the service was one way—for many, the only way—they were going to see something of the world.

Antiwar fever came late to the Mexican American community. Even after the Tet offensive convinced the rest of Middle America, the west side was still scoffing at the protesters as ungrateful.

Leaving Angie was Bert's one reservation about military service. He fully expected to marry her after June, Army or no Army. They'd been together five years, shyly holding hands at first, trading kisses after they'd walked home together.

She still wore his St. Christopher medal. Now added to the ensemble, however, was Bert's class ring, wrapped with angel hair to adjust the fit, and a pre-engagement ring. The pre-engagement ring had come soon after Angie's quinceañera, the religious and social ceremony held after her fifteenth birthday to tell the world that she was now a woman. A sort of debutante ball with mariachis. Bert had been her tuxedoed escort down the church aisle in a ceremony not unlike a wedding ceremony. He sat at the head table with her at the reception afterward, just like a groom with his bride.

Leaving her to ship out overseas bothered Bert. So when Uncle Zeke asked the question, the first pang of separation seized him. It crept into his loins and worked its way up to his chest.

"Boy, you listening?" Zeke prompted. Bert wasn't, but nodded anyway. He was thinking about Angie.

Angie, five-foot-two, was a short combination of smiles, dimples, and supple proportions. Bert was under her spell.

His friends called it being whipped—as in pussy whipped—but others might have recognized it as a surprisingly mature relationship based on trust, admiration, friendship, and love.

Bert shuffled his feet and ran his fingers through his thick black hair. He told Uncle Zeke that he'd better go find Angie.

Angie was talking to his cousin Petra—everyone called her Pete. Pete was Angie's best friend and was responsible, even if Bert didn't know it, for throwing the two together. Only Petra and Angie knew that Angie had had a crush on Bert since fourth grade and that it was the gentle hints Pete dropped into Bert's ears that sparked the romance. Bert believed it had been his masterful strategy of seduction. Angie let him continue believing.

"We're going to be opening gifts soon," Bert said, interrupting a gigglefest.

"Oh, leave us alone," said Pete. "She'd rather be with me. I'm far more interesting."

Bert smiled. "Who are you two tearing apart now?"

"Look at Tío Chuy's wife. She can't be much older than we are. Angie said she looks like the Fat Lady at the Orange Show, but with a miniskirt and more whiskers."

Indeed, the new wife was on the chunky side and was wearing a bright red miniskirt.

"I don't know. Some men like plenty of carne with their papás. If they do, you shouldn't have any problem getting a man."

Both Angie and Pete slugged Bert, who crouched into a boxing stance. "Oh, cut it out," said Pete. "I could take you with both hands tied behind your back."

"Huh?" said Bert.

Pete was Bert's favorite cousin, the only one in the family his own age. He had taught her to drive stick shift and had introduced her to any number of his friends for double dating. All of Pete's dates had so far declined to pursue a relationship, however. Outspoken, sharp-tongued, and with little tolerance for strutting peacocks, Pete was also far more intelligent and ambitious than most 14th-Street boys. She decided early that she was going away to college and was not going to get married, pregnant, and saddled with kids right when her life was supposed to be beginning.

It was a discussion near and dear to the three. Angie and Bert tried to tell her that, for them, marriage would be the beginning of their lives. Pete was just as adamant that teenage marriage was an abyss into which hopes and dreams were tossed and lost.

The argument was lost on Bert and Angie, who even now were cuddling—Bert's arm draped around Angie's shoulders and hers around his waist.

"You guys are hopeless. You deserve one another," she said to Bert and Angie. "Now, here's a real man." She grabbed Gabby as he walked by.

Gabby, hands in pockets, was torn between wanting to run around, whooping like an Apache with his seven-, eight-, and nine-year-old cousins and becoming part of the adult conversations carried on in various parts of the house and backyard.

Pete put her arm around him and gave him a big kiss on the forehead. She enjoyed making Gabby blush. "A college man. What? Maybe a doctor, lawyer, or rocket scientist."

"A baseball player is more like it," said Gabby, trying to squirm away, but not very hard.

"No, a handsome movie star who always gets the girl," said Angie, gently tugging on his ear.

Bert laughed and put Gabby in a headlock. "Handsome? No, he looks too much like Pete."

"Bert! Let go of your brother," Soledad said, poking her head out of the kitchen. "Come on. They're waiting for you in the back."

In the backyard wrapped presents sat atop a picnic table that had been there as long as the boys could remember. Next to the table was the tree from which hung the piñata that would burst open later for the younger cousins.

Pedo was wagging his butt under the limb in anticipation. These celebrations weren't lost on Pedo who, if not restrained, was apt to join the candy-grabbing, arm-swinging melee that accompanied any piñata bashing. Even if he didn't get in on that, there were always half-finished plates of cake and ice cream left by inattentive guests.

Everyone gathered around the table.

Fidel cleared his throat with another pull on his beer. "It didn't seem too long ago that we brought home this chillón," he began, putting his arm around Bert. "He's still a crybaby."

The uncles, also pulling on their beers, laughed.

"Today, look at my baby. He's out of his diapers but he still can't whip his old man," Fidel said, punching Bert's arm gently. "He's a man now. He earns his own money, and if he has any left after spending it on that tank he thinks is a hot rod or on the drive-in with Angie . . ."—Angie laughed and hid her face in Bert's chest—"then he brings home groceries and buys clothes for his brother. A man couldn't have better sons than this."

But sons could have a better father, Soledad thought, bitterly.

Fidel handed Bert the traditional first glass of beer—father to son—neither one caring much that it really wasn't Bert's first beer. Fidel hugged Bert warmly. Aunts dabbed at their eyes. Kids squirmed and shouted for Bert to open up the presents.

First came the jacket from Fidel and Soledad, a green flight jacket with a furry collar. Then came Gabby's present: a new shift knob for his car, oblong and wood-grained, with finger grips. Angie, who worked at JC Penney three days a week, had used her employee discount to get him an electric razor. Fidel joked that he wasn't man enough to shave yet. In truth, his mustache was thicker than Fidel's.

Each present was opened, each eliciting some comment from Bert or the audience.

"Now it's my turn," Bert said. A hush fell over the backyard. This was a momentous occasion. The kids never gave speeches.

"Mamá, I have to go pee-pee," said one little cousin.

"Shhhh, espérate." Wait.

"I'm not very good at making speeches. Gabby talks enough for all of us. . . ." Laughter. "But I'm proud to be part of such a family. I feel like I've been raised by all of you, and I know I learned something from each of you. From Pop, I've learned responsibility, that you're not a man if you don't take care of your own."

Soledad had to keep from rolling her eyes.

"From Mamá I've learned how to bootcher the English language. . . ." More laughter and a playful slap from Soledad. "Really, from Mamá I learned love and right from wrong from the wrong end of her broom. I don't know who got hit more, Pedo or me."

He paused, not quite certain how best to continue.

"I've got some news. I'll be finishing high school soon. I know I don't want to work in a store all my life although they've been very good to me there. Santa Fe has been good to all of us, and maybe I'll work there someday. But before I do that I want to know what's inside me. I want to see something outside of Berdoo."

Angie knew what was coming but still her stomach sank.

"I'm going to join the Army."

Tía Simona shook her head. The Navy. It should be the Navy, she thought. Henry shot her a look that said, "Don't interfere."

She returned a look that said, "Don't interfere with my interference."

Whistles and hoots from the men. More dabbing of eyes by the aunts. This was news to Soledad.

But Bert wasn't finished. "Wait. I want to say something else."

He pulled a little box out of his pocket. From it, he took a ring. "Coming home would be very special if Angie let me put this ring on her finger and said she'd be my wife."

Gritos filled the air. Angie threw her arms around his neck and kissed him long and hard. And Pete thought, "It all started with a St. Christopher medal."

The men slapped Bert on the back. They shook Fidel's hand. The women surrounded Angie for hugs and closer looks at the ring.

The cake appeared miraculously, and the women began dishing it out. No one noticed when Bert and Angie slipped away for a drive to a secluded spot for their own private celebration and further discussion about the future.

Everyone was in a festive mood except Pete, Soledad, and Gabby.

Pete was torn between joy for her best friend and favorite cousin and anguish because each of them would now be tied permanently to Berdoo and deadening mediocrity.

Soledad was in shock. Why hadn't she known? It hit her hard: she was now the second woman in two of her men's hearts.

Gabby didn't know what he was feeling. A sense of loss, he supposed. But deep in the pit of his stomach was a queasiness, a feeling of dread: things were going to change quickly and permanently.

October 13, 1967: Gabby

A Saturday for Gabby began with drudgery and ended in frivolity.

Gabby had to earn his $1.50 per week allowance. Beds had to be changed, leaves raked, a lawn mowed, a car washed. After those chores he had to attend catechism at St. Anthony's. Though he had long ago undergone his First Holy Communion and last year had completed Holy Confirmation, Soledad insisted that his sixth-grade Saturdays also be spent in a St. Anthony's classroom.

There was no avenue of appeal. Pop sat watching baseball and football games or Bullwinkle and Rocky while Soledad dragged Gabby to Sunday Mass. It was understood that, while Pop had the franchise on weekend relaxation, Mamá was in charge of religious instruction.

So Gabby and Bert learned early to make the sign of the cross when passing a church, to go to confession every week, and to never get caught throwing spitwads in church. It was a mortal sin and penance was painfully extracted when Pop heard.

The older Bert got, the more he backslid. But some of the habits were as ingrained as menudo stains on a white go-to-church shirt. He still crossed himself when passing a church and still wore his crucifix.

Gabby was perhaps the only 14th-Street youth who could recite the rosary, a skill drummed into him by Soledad. She was a woman possessed on the topic. Jesucristo and the saints had lost Fidel and Bert but were going to have a Freddie Blassie toehold on Gabby. Soledad's biggest fear was that Gabby's natural curiosity and intellect, welcome in all other areas, would lead him to other religions. She had visions of an adult Gabby shaking a tambourine and shouting "Amen" in a Holy-Roller big-top revival.

Astute Pedo could sense a Jehovah's Witness a block away. Word spread quickly among the proselytizers who worked 14th Street of the pamphlet-eating brute. Bolder missionaries would wait until another sect created a diversion, then risk martyrdom in mad dashes to the front door. The few who made it to the Rivera front door found they had better be able to speak Spanish, because, all of a sudden, Soledad forgot how to speak English.

Soledad need not have worried about Gabby. Any religion that required Saturday door-to-door proselytizing would hold no allure. It was bad enough that Saturday catechism cut into cartoon time and his ability to cavort through the neighborhood with Chuchi and Louie.

As a rule, if the chores were done and catechism dispensed with, the day was pretty much Gabby's to fill as he liked, within bounds. Gabby was expert at exceeding those bounds without detection, although he was also expert at completing chores quickly and thoroughly.

As usual on Saturday, Gabby dropped by to pick up Louie. In certain violation of federal antitrust statutes, Soledad and Mrs. Maldonado conspired to keep both boys in catechism at least through sixth grade. They reasoned that if one dropped out, it would be all that much harder to keep the other in. Since Confirmation last year, however, both boys could find no reason to go to catechism, and, although they carried their catechism missals, they rarely made it to Sister Bernadette's classroom. Their frequent absences would catch up to them eventually, but on this Saturday they didn't care.

On this Saturday, they had their BB guns, stashed the night before at Louie's house. By previous agreement, the pair were going to Little Mountain for BB-gun war.

They marched over the Muscupiabe bridge, their unloaded rifles hidden in their pants, and their pockets rattling with loose BBs. They almost resisted temptation when a Santa Fe train rumbled underneath, but not quite. BBs pinged harmlessly off the rail cars.

Gabby and Louie would have to pass through a relatively ritzy neighborhood and through several backyards to get to Little Mountain, always a dicey proposition because Anglos were antsy about little Mexicans carrying guns.

Gabby was telling Louie about Bert's big announcement the night before. "Have you seen Angie's little sister Veronica?" asked Louie. "I think she likes me."

"Aww, man. She's only in fifth grade. Next year we'll be going to Sturges with all the a-toda-madre rucas." Gabby was looking forward to junior high.

An old lady raking leaves in her front yard paused. "Sam, Sam, come here," she hissed across the yard to the garage. A plump old man in an undershirt and with a cigar in his mouth came out. She nodded toward the boys, who had unsheathed their rifles. The old man watched, waved his hand in disgust at his wife, and walked slowly back into the garage.

"Do you think he'll go to Vietnam?" Louie asked.

"I think he wants to," said Gabby. "I think he thinks that's what Pop would do."

Gabby had waited up for Bert the night before. Pop had passed out in front of the television. Mamá was still washing dishes, picking up the house, and reminding him about catechism in the morning.

Gabby and Bert shared a room. Gabby's side was cluttered with sports equipment, school books, clothes, and comic books. Bert's side was always neat. A blown-up photo of Angie hung on the wall alongside posters of cars. A small phonograph sat on a table against the wall. Underneath, 45s were neatly stacked, tributes to Bert's love affair with oldies. "Angel Baby," "Whittier Boulevard," and "Donna" played too often for Gabby's tastes.

Bert came in, beaming with self-satisfaction, much like Pedo after he'd chased a Jehovah's Witness down the street. Gabby guessed accurately that Bert had gone mano-a-mano with Angie. "You should be asleep, mocoso."

Gabby put down the *Green Lantern* comic book. "Tía Simona says the Navy is better because you can learn something," he said.

"Yeah. Just look what it did for Uncle Henry," said Bert, echoing sentiments he had often heard his father utter.

"Why?" Gabby asked, his voice cracking a bit.

"What? Marrying Angie or joining the Army?"

"The Army. There's a war going on, stoooopid."

Bert smiled, plopping down on his bed.

"Pete says you're going to get your ass shot off." Gabby whispered the last part in case Mamá was eavesdropping again. She was.

Bert considered how to explain. Pete had the right idea. San Bernardino was a trap, as if the valley bottleneck stymied personal escape in addition to capturing the L.A. smog. Pete had the initiative and the grades to get away. Bert didn't. Moreover, Bert knew he was trapped and didn't mind. Trapped was Pete's word.

Bert saw himself as being enveloped in comforting things, things he knew and trusted. Some might call it lack of ambition. Someone astute might see that Bert knew intimately who he was and where he belonged. If being trapped is the price to pay for belonging, then some might yearn for such a prison.

He could see, however, that San Bernardino afforded some tests but not others. Bert had already passed every test San Bernardino had to offer and still didn't know if he was a man. He didn't know if he was as much a man as Fidel.

Fidel's brand of machismo was, in subtle form, a challenge. He worked hard for his family and, by questioning what Bert did with his time and money, challenged him to do better.

After Bert's Little League and Pony League games, Fidel had razzed Bert for the missed balls and his errors; he got a pat on the back for any hit or home run.

Bert remembered the razzing.

If someone had told Fidel that he was encouraging his sons to compete with him, he would have scoffed, or he would have explained it as part of a time-honored, common-sense tradition of daring children to be better. Truth was, Fidel was just too damned competitive.

"When Pop tells us about Korea, what do you think he's saying?" Bert asked Gabby.

"I don't know. He's just telling us how it was and maybe bragging a little bit so we can be proud of him," Gabby said after some thought.

"Yeah, I know. But what do you think he's really saying?" Bert insisted. "He's saying that when he was about my age, he was given a test, and how he handled that test decided whether or not he would go on to the next stage of his life— for him, his life with Mamá and us. Sometimes I think he's saying that you deserve only what you earn."

Gabby snorted. "I think it's mostly beer talking. Jesus, Bert, he was drafted."

Bert laughed. "Go to sleep, mocoso. You don't under-stand."

"I understand more than you think. I understand you want to be a man before your time."

That astonished Bert. "Is that Pete talking or you?"

"Mamá. You made her cry."

Mamás never want their hijos to leave, Bert thought. Still, he was saddened. He hadn't thought how his surprise an-nouncement would affect Soledad. All he remembered was the pride in Fidel's eyes and the warm hug he'd been given. But Gabby saw the tears in Soledad's eyes. He always had been more Soledad's son than Fidel's.

Gabby was thinking of her tears while he scaled the last backyard fence on the way to Little Mountain. He and Louie trudged up the utility road to the small hill's summit.

"Ever since the Orange Show, Chuchi's not been with us much," Louie observed. After the Orange Show melee, the Lords had taken Chuchi in, impressed by his bravado and toughness. He was about to become the youngest member ever.

"Look, there's one," said Gabby, pointing at turds of unknown origin. Flies swarmed around the pile. That's how Gabby and Bert honed their marksmanship. They'd plink flies with their BB guns.

Gabby and Louie loaded their rifles. Gabby took the first shot. The BB plopped into the turd, and a surprised fly lay buried underneath, a fitting burial if you thought about it.

After a while Louie and Gabby tired of shooting flies.

It was time for BB war.

The rules were simple: find cover and shoot, get closer, and then pepper the opponent as fast as the lever action could work. The game lasted until no more BBs were left or until someone went home crying. Gabby and Louie were good enough friends that neither tried for head shots, although it happened by chance often enough. Years later, Gabby would shudder at the imbecility of it all. But at eleven years old, on Little Mountain, it was just plain fun. The adrenaline pumped, the heart raced. Pretty soon the BBs didn't even hurt.

Gabby crawled through a gully. Louie held the high ground, standing up straight, scanning the terrain with his rifle barrel.

Inching on his stomach, Gabby made believe he was in Vietnam. He poked his head over the gully's lip. Louie was holding his ground, now crouched to provide as small a target as possible. A dirt biker in the distance caught his attention. The motorcycle was complaining shrilly about a steep, bumpy climb.

Gabby made a crouching dash for the end of the gully.

"OK, Gabby. Come on out. I won't shoot," Louie shouted to the other end of the gully, aiming his rifle.

Gabby took aim, increasing his elevation a bit to make up for the distance. Ping. Louie yelped, wheeled, and fired a shot at Gabby. Gabby ducked for cover, coming up immediately to shoot again. Ping.

Louie dropped his rifle and grabbed his eye. "Ayyy!"

Oh, shit. Gabby dropped his gun and ran to Louie. "What's the matter?"

Louie picked up his rifle, smiling. "Man, your heart's going to get you in trouble every time."

"Wait, Louie. That's not fair. I thought you were hurt." Louie just smiled as Gabby inched back to his own rifle.

"Hold it, cabrón, or I'll shoot. Now repeat after me. Louie is the handsomest stud on 14th Street."

Gabby laughed nervously. "I don't lie. Not even under torture."

"Repeat after me. Louie is the handsomest stud on 14th and Gabby is a joto."

The rifle was aimed straight at Gabby's chest, and at that distance even Louie couldn't miss. It would hurt.

"Louie is the handsomest stud on 14th," Gabby repeated.

"And Gabby is a joto," Louie prompted.

"And . . . Louie is a joto," Gabby yelled as he hit the ground rolling. The BB caught him a grazing, but stinging, shot on the shoulder. Louie worked the lever action, but Gabby had found a weapon. The turd hit Louie square in the face.

Leaving Louie cursing in two languages, Gabby ran back to his gun and crouched in the gully.

Then began a bitter war of attrition, no quarter given, none asked. When the BBs ran out, turd and dirt-clod grenades rained. By the end of the day, Louie and Gabby were badly soiled. They also reeked.

No matter. There were swimming pools on the way home. Walking home, Gabby's thoughts turned again to Soledad.

"Mamá's acting really strange," Gabby confided.

"Whatayamean?"

"Like she's not talking much to Pop anymore. Like she's mad at him or something. You can always tell when Mom's mad cause you can't shut her up any other time."

It was true. It mattered little that Fidel mostly just grunted, she'd continue to chatter.

"What's wrong with that? My mom and dad never talk except to shout at each other or at me," Louie said. "You're lucky."

"I wonder what Pop did now?" Gabby wondered aloud. The last time Soledad got mad was at Christmas. As a matter of fact, she got mad every Christmas Eve. After she and the aunts had finished making tamales and everyone went home, Pop would come home drunk from someone else's Christmas party. Every Christmas she told him that if he came home drunk one more Christmas, he just shouldn't come home.

This last Christmas Eve, she even had Bert and Gabby wrestle the refrigerator he had bought her for Christmas onto the front lawn. That was the signal to the neighbors that Fidel was getting polluted again.

By Christmas morning, Pop could usually tease Soledad into good humor, but these days there was an edge to Mamá's anger. Gabby thought that if it weren't for Bert's birthday party, there would have been fireworks.

"Do you think it's because he's drinking a lot again?" Louie asked. Fidel's Christmas drinking bouts were infamous in the neighborhood.

"Nah. I don't think so. He hasn't been drinking any more than usual. I kinda like him drunk anyway. He can never say no when he's drunk. He doesn't get drunk enough as far as I'm concerned. If he drank more, maybe I could quit going to catechism."

Louie laughed. "We don't go to catechism now. Do you think Father O'Leary ever threw a turd?" He hadn't liked Father O'Leary ever since he had to say ten Hail Marys, ten Our Fathers, and an extra Act of Contrition after he was foolish enough to confess to jerking off. Now he just jerked off and trusted that God had gone through puberty too and understood.

They found sprinklers just down the road from Little Mountain. A blue-haired lady watched suspiciously from the window as the pair scrubbed themselves clean.

"I think it's something different. I think maybe Pop has done something really wrong."

"Maybe he has another ruca," Louie said.

"That's not funny, Louie."

"Cálmate, ése. Cálmate. I'm sorry," Louie said, holding up his hands.

But it hurt because it had already occurred to Gabby. He just wasn't ready to accept the possibility. "He probably was just arguing with one of Mamá's sisters' husbands again. He doesn't really like Tío Renaldo. He says he reminds him of Uncle Henry."

But the dread he had felt at Bert's party returned.

October 13, 1967: A Long Evening

Soledad watched passively as Fidel took his shower, put on a coat and tie, and left.

"Where?"

"Out."

Fine, she said to herself. She was going "out" too.

Ya basta. Enough, Soledad thought. There had been years of suspicions, but she now knew in her heart that Fidel was faithless. Years of compliance and rationalization had finally given way to a baser instinct: anger. She had thought to confront him immediately, but preparation for Bert's party, all the company, and Fidel's drinking had prevented her.

Later, her instincts had been to geld Fidel in his drunken sleep, so that he would awaken and shout for his "café" in falsetto.

Bert's announcement had not helped her mood a whit. The marriage was all right, she admitted. Soledad genuinely believed that Angie would make a fine daughter-in-law and wife. But his decision to join the Army caught her by surprise. She saw immediately that Bert was emulating his father. She grew angrier. Angie would be pregnant before the year was out, her hopes for a nursing career put on hold, perhaps permanently. Bert would ship out to Vietnam and might not come back. All this Soledad knew for a certainty. All because of some asinine code of machismo that caused men to be guided by their camotes—their penises—and that rendered them more sensitive than schoolgirls during their first periods.

In the name of machismo, Fidel was likely out with his puta now.

In the name of machismo, Fidel had held sway in the house for eighteen years. She had served him, had his children, boosted his ego, and loved him as best she knew how. Fidel rewarded her with deceit.

And now machismo was casting a shadow over Bert's life.

She remembered that when she was of courting age she and her sisters had viewed machismo in a different light. That macho aloofness had made Soledad and her sisters, awash in girlish insecurities, work all the harder to win their men's love.

If your man went out on you, you blamed the other woman and always took him back.

To hell with that, Soledad thought.

Fidel's camote was not so versatile that it could seduce women all on its own. No, Fidel had to work at it. For years she had tried not to think about it. He was out with his Catholic War Veterans friends, she had thought. But that was back when the puta was some faceless entity.

Dolores was flesh and blood and was too beautiful to ignore.

Tonight Soledad arranged to borrow Bert's car. Bert squawked initially. Saturday night, after all, was traditional cruising night, but something in Soledad's demeanor told Bert that tonight he was not going to argue further. He and Angie would use the old Chevy pickup truck with three speeds on the column that Angie's father drove, even if "Fernández Auto Body and Paint" was emblazoned on the doors. Soledad couldn't drive anyway.

Soledad knew just where she was going. The recreation hall of the Church of the Immaculate Conception in Colton had many a dance. She knew there was one there tonight. Simona had told her that Henry was still trying to get a date.

Soledad put on her best housedress, a flower-patterned affair. She told Gabby that he would be alone in the house for a while tonight. Gabby didn't mind. At eleven—almost twelve—he could think of something to do by himself, and he wasn't going to tell Father O'Leary about it, either.

Soledad had seen Bert drive the car a million times, had sat in the passenger seat as he shifted up for reverse and through gears one, two, three, and four, picking up speed along the way. Easy, she often told herself.

Too bad she hadn't noticed the extra pedal on the floor, pressed before each shift.

Turning the key, the car lurched backward as the motor began to turn. "¿Qué pasó?" she said aloud.

She tried again. Same thing.

Again. Same thing.

"Ay que la fregada." Shit.

Inside the house, Gabby had settled in front of the television. He had his night all mapped out. First, a little *Gilligan's Island* and *Mannix*. Then to find some of Bert's dirty magazines for some self-entertainment.

"Mijo, do you know how to drive?" Soledad asked him, poking her head through the front door.

This has possibilities, Gabby thought. "Sure, Mamá. Want me to drive you some place?"

"Do you know how to drive este fregado steeek sheeeft?"

"Yeah. Where do you want to go?"

After Gabby put on his shoes and coat, Soledad made him sit in the passenger seat.

"I need to go to Colton. Every time I start the car, it jumps backward and the engine stops."

"Lemme see," Gabby said.

She turned the key and the car lurched backward.

"Aw, Mamá. You gotta press down on the clutch. Just let me drive."

Soledad had already considered but rejected the idea. That's all she needed. To explain to la chota that, yes, her eleven-year-old son was driving, but she really did need to go to Colton to catch her husband cheating on her. He might not be a Catholic cop. "No, mijo. Is this the clutch?" She stepped down on the extra pedal.

"Yeah. Step on it and then start the car." The car turned over instantly, the glass-pack muffler rumbling ominously.

Gabby explained the shift pattern and that she had to let the clutch out slowly after each shift. She killed the engine several times trying to get out of the driveway.

Tía Simona pretended she had pressing duties in her flower garden as she watched Soledad's stop-and-go technique.

Gears grinding, tires peeling rubber in short-lived bursts of speed, the orange Chevy made its way past Simona's house. Tía Simona knew, just like the Christmas gift on the front lawn, that this too had something to do with her nephew.

"Qué brutos los hombres Rivera," she muttered to herself.

"Mamá, let the clutch out slowly when you want to go. And press on the gas slowly at the same time."

Soledad was trying. Stop lights were going to be hell.

They turned on to Mt. Vernon, Gabby pleading for Soledad to let him drive, that she was ruining Bert's car, that maybe she should time the lights better. Horns honked and people pointed and got out of the way of the crazy woman in the orange Chevy.

So far she hadn't even gone past second gear. Up the bridge over the railyard, the engine roared. Downhill, Soledad kept the clutch in, gaining too much speed and coming to a screeching halt at the bottom of the hill.

Finally, they got to Colton and the church recreation hall. Gabby was a nervous wreck and nearly in tears. "You wanted to got to a dance? Mamá, couldn't Pop take you? I'm missing *Gilligan's Island*."

"You wait here, mijo," Soledad said as she gave up trying to park and left the car in the middle of the church parking lot. Rattled, she left the key. Gabby was determined to park the car before la chota showed up. Soledad paid her three dollars at the door and disappeared inside.

Inside, Fidel and Dolores were sitting at their table, a beer in front of Fidel and a 7-Up in front of Dolores. Fidel had been petulant most of the night. Dolores had to egg him on to the dance floor. She was determined he wasn't going to ruin her good time.

When he had picked her up, he was visibly impressed with her outfit—a clingy red dress with a low neckline. She had borrowed the pearls from her sister, and the white gloves had come from Tencha.

Fidel made the standard pitch to stay in. Grabbing her by the waist, he maneuvered her back to the bedroom, Dolores protesting all the way as he kissed her, bit her neck and earlobes, and bent her back onto the bed.

Talking her out of the clinging dress, Fidel made hurried love to Dolores.

"You just looked so good," Fidel said afterward. He smelled deliciously of Old Spice and now a little bit of her.

She let him lie there for a few minutes longer and then gently nudged him off, bringing her head to rest on his hairless chest. "I spent an hour putting this makeup on," she teased.

"You put it on to turn me on. It worked," Fidel chuckled.

She got up and went into the bathroom to make another stab at the makeup.

"Why don't we just stay here?" Fidel asked.

"No, you don't. You promised to take me dancing and you're going to. Don't worry. We'll come back here and start all over again."

She had never seen Fidel pout before.

At the dance, Fidel surveyed the room constantly, on the lookout for friends and acquaintances. Why couldn't they have gone to a dance in Riverside, he thought. No one knows me there. If Henry Macías actually found a date, Fidel was in big trouble. If Henry knew, Tía Simona would know soon as well. Then Soledad. Then the entire neighborhood. His chest tightened.

Why had he let her talk him into this?

On the bandstand, a group played a combination of standards, cumbias, and norteñas.

"Vamos, Fidel. We came to dance." Dolores grabbed Fidel's arm and dragged him on to the floor for a very slow one. "Now I feel like I'm yours," Dolores whispered as they danced. "Out in public, like we should be."

One-two, one-two. Fidel tried to keep his mind on his dancing. Sort of like trying to think of baseball during sex. If you thought about baseball, you might forestall the inevitable. He was having trouble understanding all his feelings, but there was a feeling of inevitability about his relationship with Dolores.

Maybe he was in love. He had never known anyone who loved him so physically before. Soledad's love was more a mind thing, equally possessing and rewarding in other ways.

But to have a woman show him physical love was new. Not since Vera Domínguez when he was sixteen had a female let him know that he was wanted. The message he got from Soledad was not, "I love you," but "we'll do it if you want to. Anything to make you happy." Not quite the same thing. One was offered and the other done as if it were just another household chore. Even the way Dolores held him as they danced said, "I want you and I'm all yours."

"Why don't you just fuck her on the dance floor?"

Fidel froze.

Soledad stood a few paces away. Other dancers instinctively made way for her.

Fidel didn't know if he was more surprised to see her or to hear her say "fuck."

"What do you think you're doing? Where's Gabby? If you brought Gabby, I'll . . ."

"You'll what? Leave me. It looks like you've already done that. Only your body makes it to the dinner table anyway. Don't you want your son to see how much of a man his papá is? A real man cheats on his wife, and his putas spread their legs whenever he wants."

The dancers were now steering well clear. They had seen similar confrontations end in gunfire. Dolores stood open-mouthed.

"Go home, Soledad. We'll talk later. You're making a fool of yourself," Fidel urged.

"I'll go home. But let's get it straight now. It's my home, and if you come home it had better be just to get your clothes. I'm tired of all of it, Fidel. Todo!"

Dolores tried to sidle away but wasn't quick enough. "And you, you can have him. Him and his camote. You can wash his calzones, cook his meals, and maybe someday you can come to a dance and see him fucking someone else on the dance floor."

Soledad was crying, the tears streaming down her face. Dolores was crying too, mascara running in dark streaks. Only Fidel was stone-cold calm. "Go home and maybe if you're lucky I'll come home. I pay the bills, cabrona. I'll come and go as I please."

He hadn't noticed Gabby standing next to his mother, just in time to hear his pop call his mamá a cabrona.

A rent-a-chota tugged at Soledad's coat, trying to coax her away.

"Let go of Mamá," Gabby said, pulling at the cop's arm. Fidel tried to intercede. Gabby turned on him. "You leave her alone too. I used to want to be like you. Now, I'd rather be like Pedo. At least he's honest about his screwing."

Fidel made like he was going to backhand Gabby, but then lowered his arm. Gabby's eyes shone with pure malevolence.

"Take your mother home, Gabby. You don't know what you're saying."

Gabby escorted a sobbing Soledad off the dance floor away from the staring strangers. The most remote stranger of all was his father, he thought.

Soledad didn't protest when Gabby got in the driver's seat. Bert had taught him to drive long ago; the seat moved all the way forward so his feet could reach the pedals.

Soledad's sobs sliced through Gabby all the way home. "Don't cry, Mamá. Things will be all right. You'll see. Pop will come back and promise to be good."

"I don't know if I want him to come back, mijo. I don't know that man. He's not the man I married." She knew as she said it that Fidel was the same and that Dolores was just one in a long line of deceits. It was Soledad who had changed. Once she had seen Dolores, she knew she would have to change or lose all self-respect.

It was easier not knowing or, rather, pretending not to know.

From now on, Soledad thought, she would be no man's fool.

As the orange Chevy glided into the driveway, Soledad made herself a promise: time to grow up; a woman who serves a man who mistreats her is just a whore of a different sort.

The Same Evening

The strangers whispered. Some snickered as Fidel and Dolores left the dance.

"He can't handle his woman."

"Puta," from the women.

Fidel didn't know which was worse, being humiliated in front of his mistress or in front of his son. Gabby's basketball rolled in the back of the station wagon on the return to Dolores's house, every thump a reminder that his world had just been jostled.

"She has a house. Children. She doesn't know when she has it good. Vieja cabrona. She has all she wants. I get nothing I need. If it wasn't for me, she'd still be barefoot in Zacatecas, feeding the pigs."

Seeing the hurt in Gabby's eyes pained him.

"She just lays there like we're doing something dirty."

Before today, Fidel had expected unquestioned adoration from his wife and sons. Respect.

Driving past Nuñez Park, he remembered a Saturday afternoon long ago when the park was called Gateway Park. The soccer game had been raucous and unusually physical. Fidel had scored a goal. He had played the game when he was a kid at this park and had been reintroduced to fútbol by Soledad's immigrant brothers, who talked him into joining a league with them.

Mexican Americans didn't like to admit it, but there was deep resentment of newly arrived brethren. "Cabeza de Mexicano" was a common enough term in the Rivera household, directed at anyone thought to lack common sense or to act like a country bumpkin. Fidel and his brothers routinely derided the "mojados" on Mt. Vernon, easily recognizable by their plain dress and confused looks. Fidel overcame some of those biases when he married into Soledad's family, most of whom had since followed her to the United States, legally and illegally. He overcame enough of the prejudice, anyway, to play soccer every Saturday when Bert and Gabby were younger with as many mojados as it took to field two teams. "La Migra," immigration, could have made a pretty good haul had they thought of it.

On this particular Saturday, Fidel was doing well at moving the ball, angering the opposition because they thought the referees were blatantly ignoring fouls and illegal use of hands. They were right. The referees worked with Fidel at Santa Fe. Gabby and Bert jumped up and down on the sidelines when he scored his goal. They often accompanied Fidel to the games while Soledad stayed home doing laundry.

After the game, when the traditional beer cooler was opened, one of the losing team members walked up to Fidel and told him what he thought of his sportsmanship, his lineage, and his wife's sexual habits. It was all in Spanish, but even Fidel knew that he had been insulted.

So Fidel dropped his beer and broke the other player's nose, clearing both benches and causing a general melee stopped only by the intercession of Father Nuñez from nearby Our Lady of Guadalupe. The padre lost a new pair of eyeglasses in the fracas.

On the way home, Bert and Gabby relived the fight blow by blow. "One-punch Pop," Bert had named Fidel, who told the boys not to mention the altercation to their mother. His chest swelled anyway when he later heard Gabby spill the story to Soledad about how "Pop beat up the other team."

Now, Fidel thought, that respect was gone.

"The boy has got to learn," Fidel mumbled. "A los hombres todos los derechos. A las mujeres las lágrimas." For men, the rights. For woman, the tears. Something he heard his mother say often.

Fidel remembered when he first learned of his own father's

indiscretions from a friend. He confirmed his father's relationship with a widow across Mt. Vernon during a spying mission. He never told his mother. But he knew she knew, though she had the good grace to pretend she didn't.

Soledad could have learned some lessons from that woman, Fidel thought.

Dolores was silent. She understood that to join in the denunciation of her rival would be viewed as shrill and might even prompt a stirring defense from Fidel. She recognized an opportunity but couldn't help feeling a little sorry for Soledad. Feminist solidarity in this kind of matter was then as rare in Mexican culture as a Republican in a soup kitchen.

Still, Dolores knew shit when she saw it. Self-interest won out, however.

"Papacito. Why don't you spend the night?" she said, sidling next to him.

"It's my house. I pay the bills. I'm not going to be kicked out of my own house," he thundered.

"It's just for the night. Tomorrow, maybe she'll not be as angry."

"I don't give a goddamn how she feels."

Fidel was staying out a little longer, however, to make the point to Soledad about his independence. He thought he knew Soledad well enough to know that she would find living with his many faults preferable to living without him. Years of living with servility had not bred in Fidel the expectation that someday he might not be served. So, in a fit of defiance, he and Dolores went for a beer at El Chino's. It was all out in the open now.

Dolores beamed as she walked into the restaurant on Fidel's arm. Mr. Lu's eyes bugged out, but he said nothing. Fidel ordered two beers. The night waitress and Dolores exchanged looks and barely suppressed girlish giggles.

Dolores wasn't the only El Chino girl to score. Henry Macías and Tencha sat together at another table.

"What's going on?" Henry asked Tencha.

"Dolores got her man," Tencha answered simply, wondering if there was some easy way to cut this evening short.

In the background, the jukebox whined a sad song of love. "Albur de amor. Me gustó. Yo lo jugué." I played the game of love. "Cómo era pobre yo." Poor me.

*   *   *

At home, Soledad sat in the kitchen, the refrigerator Fidel had given her four Christmases ago gently humming, Pedo on the floor beside her. Gabby had cried until no more tears came. Now, lying on his bed, he shuddered periodically in a restless sleep.

Soledad hoped his demons would be gone when he awoke but didn't really believe it. She was also done crying. In front of her was the family checkbook and savings passbook.

She and Fidel never discussed finances. It was understood that, although her name was on both accounts, it was only a formality. Any money she made from her sewing went for groceries and other incidental household expenses. She never saw Fidel's paycheck, didn't know how much money he made or whether they were rich or poor. She never thought to ask.

The checkbook lay open in front of her but it might as well have been written in Mayan hieroglyphics. The last entry was for $33.54. She didn't know if that was a balance, a deposit, or a notation for a check written. She knew a bit about checks.

The savings book was a little simpler. The last entry was for $7,262. It wasn't in Fidel's distinctive scrawl so Soledad guessed some bank clerk wrote in how much the Riveras had in savings. It seemed like a lot.

Soledad grew angrier. Her washing machine was fifteen

years old, and she still had to hang clothes on a line outside because Fidel said they couldn't afford a dryer.

Bert wasn't home and Soledad considered waking Gabby to decipher the financial code, but she knew Gabby had been through enough.

Guilt. She hadn't intended to drag Gabby through the marital blowout. It pained her that Gabby might think less of his father. That's what she told herself. In her heart she was grateful for an ally.

Soledad was laying the groundwork for independence. Out of anger, self-respect might grow.

The concept was totally alien. Soledad grew up in an environment that taught her that her worth was measured by how much she could please and nurture. Picking up men's calzones off the floor was second nature. She had done it for her father and brothers and now did it for her husband and sons.

At family gatherings when she was a girl, she remembered her mother telling her and her sisters to see if her brothers, male cousins, and uncles needed anything. The women stayed in the kitchen.

There had been little resentment.

Soledad wondered if she could take care of herself. How silly, she thought, a grown woman forced to wonder if she could care for herself and what remained of her family. As she looked at the financial records, Soledad had reason to doubt her abilities.

Pedo's ears perked up. Soon, Soledad knew, she would hear Fidel's station wagon come up the driveway. So much for making her threat stick. Soledad supposed she could take Gabby and trudge off to one of her sisters' houses, but she would have to ask Fidel to drive her.

Fidel's keys jangled at the front door.

Pedo greeted him, waiting for his customary scratching behind both ears and brief wrestling match. Fidel stalled just long enough for Soledad to finish putting the financial records away in the kitchen junk drawer.

Her eyes never left him as he went to the refrigerator and slipped out a Burgie. Maybe, just maybe, if Soledad hadn't shamed him in front of his son and all those strangers, he might have come home contrite and asking forgiveness.

"Don't say a thing. Don't say a goddamn thing," Fidel said, never looking at her as he rummaged for a can opener. "Where's the goddamn can opener? Goddammit, you can never find anything in this house."

A whisper.

"What did you say?" Fidel asked.

"I said, do you know what Fidel means?" Soledad said softly.

"What are you talking about? Of course I know what my name is."

Soledad shook her head violently, trying hard to stem the flow of angry tears. "Your name, Fidel. It means faithful," she said, staring at him through red, teary eyes.

Fidel stopped in the doorway for a second. He walked to the living room and turned on the television, but he didn't much notice what was on. He looked at the trophy rack, filled with school letters, Little League trophies, academic certificates. The Hamm's Beer wall sign—the cascading waterfall was turned on only for benefit of company—told Fidel of the "Land of Sky Blue Waters."

Fidel knew what his name meant. Goddammit. If going to work every day, coming home most nights, making sure his children were cared for and that his wife had someone to grow old with wasn't being faithful, he didn't know what was.

He sat on the couch, staring blankly at the television.

Soledad whispered through the doorway, "Did you think the calzones picked themselves up? Was it magic when they appeared in your drawer, sin la cagada?"

"Washing and folding clothes? Is that all there is to taking care of your man? You shouldn't be surprised that I went out and found someone who loved me." He shook his head, got up, and switched the channel.

"You bastard."

The word surprised Soledad almost as much as it shocked Fidel. He stopped flipping channels in the middle of the Million Dollar Movie. This week it was a creature feature, *Rodan*.

"Bastard?" Fidel peered at her through narrowed eyes. "If you were a man, I'd split your head for you."

"If you were a man, you wouldn't screw around on your wife. What kind of man builds with one hand and tears down with the other?"

"Yes, I've built something. But it's a house without a heater. There's no warmth in what I've built. There's no warmth in you. Do you know what it's like to lie next to someone, want that person, and not even know if you are wanted in return? Was it ever, even once, your idea to make love? Have you ever wanted to make love?"

Soledad sat down on the couch and stared at Fidel. "I'm talking about your family coming apart and you're talking about your camote? You've never complained and neither have I. When have I ever told you no?"

"Dammit, woman. Not saying 'no' isn't the same as saying 'yes.' I'm talking about a little affection, a reason to stay home. This is stupid," Fidel said. "The woman's supposed to complain about never hearing 'I love you.' You not only don't say it, you don't show it."

Soledad sat, mouth agape, trembling with anger. "Not showed it? Not showed it? Do you think I've had two of your children and tried to carry three others and lost them because I like big bellies, screaming babies, and pain? Look around you. Do you see any dust? Anywhere? Are there any dirty dishes in the sink? Do I just stay home and grow fat?"

Fidel flared, "That's not love. That's duty. That's what you do to keep a roof over your head."

Soledad got up and walked back toward the kitchen, then stopped and whirled around. "And you? What love have you shown me? Do you know I've never even seen your paycheck? And your idea of making love? It's running your hands over my body a few times, lifting my nightgown, and climbing on top. If you don't like the way I make love, blame yourself. You taught me. There was no one before you. But if you don't quit your puta, there will be others after you."

"This is my house and I won't be the one leaving if that's what you're thinking. There's the door if you want to use it." Fidel pointed at the door. Standing next to it was Gabby.

"Go to bed, mijo," Fidel said.

"Are you kicking Mamá out?"

"Go to bed, mijo," this time from Soledad.

"If she goes, I go," Gabby said simply, turning around and returning to his room.

February 21, 1968:
Bert, Angie, and Chuchi

Bert maneuvered the pickup truck slowly down E Street. Angie snuggled into his side. It was Saturday night, and the four-lane boulevard was bumper to bumper. Up E Street to 5th, a left on 5th and down Arrowhead to 6th and back to E. Down E to the newer McDonald's. According to local lore, Berdoo was home to the original McDonald's. Up and back and back again. All night or until the police started culling the cruisers, using curfew as an excuse.

Most rode in parents' cars, an assortment of four-doors, polished bright for the night. The cars were washed thoroughly beforehand, even if they would later be soiled with beer, liquor, and vomit stains, and littered with discarded marijuana roaches, smoked down to the nub by singed-fingered youths.

"A church wedding? Angie, let's just go to Las Vegas." Bert was teasing. He knew Angie and Petra had been planning a church wedding since she and Bert traded St. Christopher medals in junior high.

Angie paid no attention. "I want all the men in the party to wear gray tuxes with black trim. Like Sonya and Ernie, remember?" Her older brother had married soon after high school and joined the Air Force.

"Are you sure you want to join the Army, Bert? The closest they could station you is Fort Ord by San Francisco. The farthest they could send you is . . ."

There was too much planning to do to get depressed.

After Bert and Angie had slipped away from his birthday party months before, they had sealed their pact for por vida togetherness. Bert had made a passionate argument that, since they were going to be married anyway, there was little need to be careful, no need to use a rubber or pull up short of ecstasy. It was a hard sell.

"Bert, I want to fit into that white wedding dress. A swollen belly just won't do. Can't you just wait a little longer, sweetie?"

But Bert was amorously insistent. He was about to insert himself, but she stopped him.

"You better understand what this means," Angie said. "I own you. You're mine and it's a lifetime deal."

"I've been yours for longer than you know," he said.

The next day, he would have a hickey, a badge of honor and something for Soledad to scold him about.

Driving down E Street, Bert was remembering that night. He wanted more of the same tonight. Since that time, Angie had had second thoughts and had panicked when she missed her period. The period eventually came, but the panic remained.

"You know, I think I want all girls," Bert said. "Three of them."

Angie smiled but said nothing.

Since the engagement, Bert had started noticing young mothers. Angie was nearly perfect, short but well proportioned. Still, she could use a few more pounds, he thought. Bert particularly noticed that the young mothers, with children riding on hips or in strollers, filled out their jeans nicely. He envisioned Angie rounding out with the pleasing plumpness of young motherhood.

Angie noticed Bert's new interest. Jealous at first because she thought Bert was just looking at other women, she soon noticed that they were all young mothers. She was secretly pleased.

"Well, just how soon do you want these three girls? I don't want to be pregnant and have a baby while you're someplace else. And I want to go to nursing school too, you know."

Bert left it alone. He didn't want to reopen an argument about the Air Force versus the Navy versus the Army. The Air Force, as far as Bert was concerned, was just the Navy without the water—sanctuary for those unsure of their manhood.

"Bert."

"Huh?"

"Don't ever stop touching me."

"What? Right now? Can I park first? What are you talking about?"

"I mean after we're married. I don't want you to stop touching me."

Bert glanced at her. Leering, he said, "Of course I'll never stop touching you."

"No," said Angie. "Have you noticed that a lot of people, after they get married, act like they're not? Sort of like your mom and dad."

"Jesus, Angie. They have two kids, don't they?"

Angie shook her head. "I know. It's just that sometimes they don't really act like they're in love. I want us to be in love and act like it. I don't want us to grow so used to each other that the only time you touch me is when you . . . want to make babies."

"You don't have anything to worry about. I could never stop loving you. I could never stop touching you. And talking about touching, why don't we go park somewhere?"

Angie laughed and buried her head in his arm.

"I don't think Daddy's truck has enough room. And if you're thinking I'm going to get in the back on that hard floor, you're crazy."

"Well, you know I don't have to be on top all the time."

Angie blushed but was intrigued.

"Well, maybe, but I'm not easy. I want a burrito, fries, and a large Coke. And afterward, I want to go to Dairy Queen for a hot fudge.

"You sure you're not pregnant?"

In San Bernardino, if you wanted a fast-food burrito, you had your choice. Taco Bell served seasoned hamburger meat in a thin, tepidly warm flour tortilla and called it a burrito. But El Burrito on Baseline served the real thing. Their taco shells weren't industrial strength. It was about the only place to go for Mexican fast food with some assurance it was sorta Mexican.

The differences were lost on most Anglos in San Bernardino, who ate hamburger and cheesefood in rolled-up tortillas smothered in multipurpose red sauce and called it ethnic dining. But that was OK. It just meant that those people stayed on their own side of the freeway. West-side Mexicans thanked the saints that La Mitla and Alta's on Mt. Vernon hadn't been discovered.

On the other hand, neither Bert nor Gabby had ever eaten Chinese food. Bert reached his eighteenth year without ever having eaten white rice. Say rice to Bert and he thought arroz. Say sweet-and-sour pork and he likely would have scrunched up his face and sung the virtues of pork chunks, fried with onions and coated in a light chile verde. Soledad's fat homemade tortillas—those that survived Gabby as he stood next to the stove and voraciously devoured them—sopped up the chile nicely.

The pickup truck slid into its parking space in front of the square red building. El Burrito was technically on the Anglo side of the freeway, but the west side still claimed it. Bert parked next to a primer gray '55 Chevy, slung low to the ground. Inside, some Lords passed beers and burritos. Lords were a fact of life. So were fever blisters. Both were equally difficult to ignore.

"Do you have to park here?" Angie whispered as Bert turned off the engine.

"It'll be OK."

Bert got out of the car, careful to avoid eye contact with the Lord on the passenger side.

"Hey, chula," said the passenger-side Lord to Angie. One arm drooped out of the car, beer can in hand.

Bert turned around slowly and walked back. Angie shook her head violently.

The Lord saw Bert coming, turned his head, and whispered something to the others in the car. There was laughter.

"You know, vato," said Bert. "We're not looking for trouble but if your Mamá hasn't taught you how to treat ladies, I can give you some lessons."

The Lord jerked open the door and got out drunkenly. Others piled out on the other side.

"Bert. It's OK. C'mon," Angie said desperately.

"You're one of those Chancellor jotos, aren't you?" said the Lord.

Bert was wearing his Chancellor jacket.

"So you can read a little bit, huh?"

"I can kick your ass too."

"You think you can do it by yourself? You probably can't even wipe your ass by yourself."

"Bert!" Angie was afraid.

Bert probably had ten pounds and at least three inches on the Lord, but was keenly aware that, for all his bravado, he was about to wet his pants as three other Lords came around his back.

From inside the car came a familiar, deep voice.

"Cálmanse, vatos. He's one of ours."

Chuchi stepped out of the car. "Sorry, man, I didn't recognize you in that pickup truck."

Bert often heard his mother fume about Chuchi and how he was a bad influence on Gabby, but at this moment he felt like hugging him.

The offending Lord still glared at Bert.

Chuchi put his hand on his shoulder, jerked him close,

and whispered something in his ear. The Lord lowered his eyes and got in the car.

Bert recognized this for what it was—an indication that, though Chuchi was younger than the other Lords, he was already a power in the organization. He undoubtedly had had to stomp a few heads to do that.

"Hey, Chuchi. ¿Qué pasó?" What's happening?

"Aquí, nomás." Not a whole lot.

The other Lords got back into the car.

"Let's go, Chuchi," said one.

"You vatos go ahead. I'm going to catch a ride home with Bert.

"Sure, man. Hop in," Bert said. "You hungry? Want a burrito?"

"I ain't got no money," said Chuchi, lowering his eyes and sticking his hands into his jacket pockets.

"Chicken, pork, or beef?"

"Pork."

Chuchi went around to the other side of the pickup. Angie scooted to the middle and Chuchi climbed in. As they waited for Bert, neither said anything. Angie had seen Chuchi around with Gabby but had not imagined he was old enough to be a Lord.

Chuchi could tell Angie was upset. "You mad or something?"

"Not at you. Bert. He could've got killed."

Chuchi laughed. "So you're mad because he didn't get killed?"

"It's not funny, Chuchi. If I wasn't here, he probably would have walked away from it. But it's like he thinks he's got something to prove when I'm around."

Chuchi nodded. "And if he walked away? You wouldn't think of him any different? And if those pendejos in the car wanted to go farther with you, should he have walked away from that too?"

"That's different," said Angie.

"Not really. It's sorta like he does have something to prove. If he walked away, next time the Lords saw him, he wouldn't be able to walk away. They wouldn't have killed him, just kicked his butt. But he would have hurt enough of us so that the next time we saw him, he'd be OK."

Angie turned to look at Chuchi. He seemed older than fifteen.

Bert got in the car with the burritos. "I haven't seen you around much. Where you been?"

"Just hanging out with the carnales," Chuchi said, diving into the burrito.

"Gabby misses you."

"I miss the chamaco too. I hear you and Angie are getting married. I ran into Louie the other day."

Bert nodded, his mouth full of chicken burrito.

"In August. I'm going into the Army too. I'm going to sign up this month." Glancing sideways, he noticed Angie was just staring straight ahead.

Chuchi said simply, "She thinks you should have just walked away."

Bert cursed under his breath.

"You could've gotten hurt if it wasn't for Chuchi," Angie said, tears in her eyes. "You didn't even thank him."

Chuchi laughed. "I remember a time at the Orange Show and some chingazos between the Imperials and the Lords," he said, recalling how Bert pulled him, Gabby, and Louie from police billy clubs and pointy Imperial shoes.

Angie had heard about this. "I don't want to say anything against your carnales, Chuchi, but . . . but why are you hanging out with them?"

"They're OK. Besides, someone like me doesn't have a lot of choice."

"Whatayamean?" Bert asked.

Chuchi wanted to change the subject. "Have you ever wondered how me and Gabby got to be friends?"

"I thought you just met at school."

Chuchi laughed. "I don't go to school enough to know anyone." Chuchi had had a tough reputation at Roosevelt, where all 14th-Street youth attended elementary school. The oldest sixth grader in school history, he had made up in street smarts what he lacked in book learning. He had made a practice of "borrowing" lunch money from his classmates, nobody really expecting to be repaid and nobody really willing to see what would happen if the loan were refused.

One day he tried to borrow money from Gabby, then a fourth grader. Gabby told him that he had no money, but then sat down at a lunch table and invited Chuchi to join him. He split his chorizo taco with Chuchi. He gave Chuchi half his twinkie too. So began what had been, until recently, a close friendship.

Gabby was the first friend ever invited to the Romero home. When Gabby got there, he understood a lot about his new friend. Chuchi's mother was drunk, snoring on the couch. Chuchi's latest "tío" was snoring in the bedroom. A couple of younger half brothers were rummaging through a near-empty refrigerator.

After that, Chuchi ate a lot at the Rivera household.

"I'll check in on Gabby tomorrow. Is he going to be home?" asked Chuchi.

As they drove home, Angie rested her head on Bert's shoulder. Chuchi stared out the window, wondering if rumors of trouble in the rock-solid Rivera household were true. If they were, he had a lot to teach Gabby. He would teach Gabby that life would be full of tíos who at first made his mother laugh. Later, they would make her cry.

Chuchi had grown up too fast, too hard.

May 3, 1968

In 1968, Army, Navy, Marine, and Air Force recruiters were hungry.

About the only service not hard up at the time was the Coast Guard. Join the Coast Guard and you almost certainly didn't go to Nam.

The draft was still around, but the draft didn't meet the quotas needed to build the largest post-WWII Army in U.S. history. Domino theory held sway. The fear of communism was omnipresent, unabated by the antiwar protests in the streets, and certainly not tempered by the presidential campaign of longtime commie baiter Richard Nixon.

So, when Bert stepped into the storefront recruiting office on D Street, recruiters held their breaths. "Please, oh, please, let him step this way," they all thought.

But Bert knew where he wanted to go. "I want to see the Army recruiter," he told the receptionist.

"Shit," thought the Navy, Air Force, and Marine recruiters.

"Hi, I'm Sergeant Benny Sánchez." The recruiter held out his hand. "Or just Sergeant Benny, if you want."

Posters on the walls heralded the virtues of the Army. Green-fatigued soldiers said, "Join the Army. Be a man." Exotic locales beckoned. Soldiers struck poses in the trades they'd learned—auto mechanics, electronics, communications, parachuting, driving tanks—thanks to the Army.

Their sales pitch was wasted on Bert.

"Hi. I want to join the Army."

The sergeant sized up Bert. He saw a bit of himself. Mexican, maybe not even out of high school. Maybe his girlfriend is pregnant. It wasn't a court referral or else he would have had advance notice. "Well, you came to the right place. Are you out of high school?"

"No, sir. Just about," said Bert. "But I heard about something called deferred enlistment, where I sign up now, maybe get in as E-2, and don't have to report until after graduation."

Sergeant Benny knew some other Army recruiter working a high-school career fair had done his job well. "Yeah, we have that. But if you're not eighteen, we'll still need your parents to sign."

"I'm eighteen," Bert said.

"Órale," the sergeant thought.

They hadn't even sat down yet. "Please, have a seat," Benny said.

Bert looked at the sergeant. Brown, like me, he thought.

Sergeant Benny looked good in crisply pressed khaki. The stripes said E-6, staff sergeant. Even Bert knew that. The white walls didn't detract a bit from Sergeant Benny's thick head of hair. Ribbons of many colors were pinned on his shirt above his heart. He looked lean, despite his stocky shoulders.

Sergeant Benny was a veterano: two tours in Vietnam and a request in for a third. He wanted to recruit Bert, but Sergeant Benny wasn't out to fill a quota. A minor wound from his last tour and his poster-perfect Latino appeal spelled recruiting duty. The Army was very aware that many of its GIs these days were Latino.

Sergeant Benny, however, had seen things the other recruiters hadn't. He'd seen body bags with brown-skinned youth like Bert in them. Good-looking boys before they'd stepped on land mines or been shot, their faces frozen in eternal agony. Sergeant Benny was recruiting because he loved the Army and because he followed orders, but he wasn't going to lie to the boy. "Why do you want to join the Army?" he asked.

The question caught Bert off guard. He thought he could just walk in and sign up, but the dark brown, piercing eyes demanded an answer.

"I don't know." Bert thought briefly of feeding the sergeant a line of bullshit. Maybe something like he wanted to fight for his country, or he wanted to learn a trade. He glanced at the sergeant's furrowed brow and decided on the truth.

"Well, I guess it's like this. My father was in the Army. He always said it made a man out of him. I want to be like my father. I guess that's part of it. In my family it's just what Rivera men do. And, you know, I really don't want to spend two years at Valley College just to learn how to work on cars. I've been in school for eighteen years. I'm not very good at it. I want to know what I'm good at. I like Berdoo, but I don't know that I want to stay here all my life. Or if I do, I want to be able to say I've seen and done something else."

Sergeant Benny remembered another recruiting station in nearby Barstow and a Mexican youth anxious to test himself against the world. Benny's father was a WWII vet who had returned, like Bert's Korean-vet father, to a better world than he left. Benny's youth—much like Bert's—was spent happily listening to stories of faraway places. Benny understood Bert's desire to follow in his father's footsteps.

"You know, it isn't easy," the sergeant said. "Not everyone gets the glory. Not everyone likes the Army." God, what was he saying. Was he trying to talk a recruit out of signing?

"Tell me what's it like," Bert said with curiosity.

Benny thought back. He had been a cocky kid when he joined. Kind of loco, his friends said. There were a lot of fights, mostly over inconsequential matters, though it didn't seem so at the time. A girl. A nasty look. Benny had been eager enough—too eager, his friends said—to give a bruising and to take one.

"I don't know you at all, Bert, but I'll tell you how it was with me. What you say about your father was true for me. I felt the same about wanting to leave Barstow—that's where I'm from—and test myself. But it was something different with me. I was loco. You know what that means?"

Bert nodded.

"I fought a lot about nothing. I wasn't interested in school. I didn't even finish school. I got my G.E.D. in the Army. As wild as I was, I knew I needed discipline. I wasn't going to learn it in Barstow. I knew what was going to happen. Some ruca was going to get pregnant. I was going to do the right thing and marry her. Or maybe I wouldn't and break my mother's heart. Maybe I'd work at Santa Fe, drink beer, get fat. Maybe someone would make me angry, I'd fight, and I'd go to prison. None of that sounded good to me."

Bert hadn't expected such honesty. He certainly didn't expect to hear words like "ruca" and "loco" from an Army sergeant.

"Anyway, the Army taught me discipline. Gave me confidence—the right kind. It gave me something to do that I could be proud of."

"Have you been to Vietnam?" Bert asked in a whisper.

"Yes. Twice."

Bert waited for Benny to continue. He wasn't sure he was going to. But Benny looked at Bert and said, "Don't think you're going to win glory there. It can be nasty. It's what soldiers do, and if you can't live or die with that, you shouldn't join the Army." Benny couldn't believe he was giving the boy such unvarnished truth and wondered if he had scared the youth off.

But Bert said, "No, I want to join."

The two talked a bit more. Bert wanted a favor.

"Sergeant, there's just one thing. I know I'm eighteen and I can sign up for myself, but I want my parents to understand. It's not so much my pop as my mom. She doesn't understand. All she knows is that her baby's going away. She says I'm 'tonto.' " Bert glanced at Benny to see if he understood. Benny smiled. He did. "And she says if I have to join, why not the Navy like my uncle Henry. Learn a trade. You know?"

Sergeant Benny nodded.

"Would you come to talk to them? I think they'd like you."

Benny understood that Bert was thanking him for his honesty and doing him an honor. "Sure, you just tell me when."

As they talked some more, Benny's thoughts strayed intermittently to loco times in Barstow. They seemed tame now compared to the utter chaos of the vicious war he had fought in twice and looked forward to fighting in again.

May 5, 1968

Sergeant Benny had been through the neighborhood before. He had come to the west side in search of the perfect burrito, platter of carnitas, or bowl of menudo as well as on other recruiting forays. When he crossed the large hump that took 16th Street over the freeway, it felt like coming home. The small tract houses were the same kind as in Barstow— big enough and plenty grand enough for first-time home buyers who had not expected to own a house at all. Farther west, past Mt. Vernon, was the historic barrio with wooden houses instead of stucco.

Benny pulled up to Bert's house. The flashy orange Chevy must be the boy's, he thought. Benny drove an official U.S. Army vehicle, its puke green color standing out among the whites, primer gray, and wilder colors of barrio carruchas.

Children playing on front lawns stopped to watch. Eyes peered from windows. Such a car could mean someone had died. Someone in uniform, if they weren't from the neighborhood, could be a bearer of bad news. Everyone relaxed, particularly Tía Simona, who was watering her front lawn, when the car stopped in front of the Rivera's. Everyone knew they had no family in the service.

Pedo barked, but Sergeant Benny could tell from the wagging butt that the dog posed no danger.

"Hey, chhhttt." Fidel was telling Pedo to shut up. The dog wagged his butt some more but quit barking.

Sergeant Benny extended his hand. "Hi, I'm Sergeant Benny Sánchez."

"Pase." Come in, said Fidel, shaking the sergeant's hand.

Tía Simona was still watering the lawn with a hose. Why didn't his tía buy one of those back-and-forth sprinklers like everyone else? Fidel guessed the watering gave Simona more time to spy.

The sergeant stepped into a brightly furnished room. "This is my wife, Soledad," Fidel said, gesturing to a pretty woman who, Benny could tell, had put on makeup and combed her hair for his arrival. Her neat print dress also told Benny that this was a special occasion for the family. She looked nice, Benny thought.

"Buenas tardes," Soledad said, motioning for Benny to sit down. "I'll get the boys."

Bert came in with Angie, and Gabby shuffled in behind.

"A beer, sergeant?"

"Gracias, no."

"Una coca?" A Coke? asked Soledad.

"OK," said the sergeant.

Fidel began. "Bert says he wants to join the Army. That's good, I think. His jefita is kinda worried though," he said, looking at Soledad. She returned a cold stare but turned and smiled at the sergeant.

A nice smile, Benny thought.

"So I guess you should tell us about the Army. I was in during Korea," Fidel added, obviously proud of that fact and wanting to share it.

Benny handed out some brochures. There wasn't enough room on the couch covered with colorful blankets. Fidel looked like he had been born to the reclining easy chair. Gabby brought in kitchen chairs.

"Well, Bert tells me he wants to join on deferred enlistment."

A puzzled look from Soledad told Benny he shouldn't use big words—not in English anyway.

"He wants to sign up now, but we won't take him until after he graduates."

Soledad nodded. "Will he go to the war?"

Fidel and Bert both rolled their eyes, but Angie and Soledad hung on Benny's words.

Benny looked into Soledad's eyes and knew better than to lie. "I won't lie to you. He might. It depends on how he does on his tests. He can tell us now if he wants to sign up for some specialty, like auto mechanics or electronics."

Soledad's hopes jumped.

"But if he doesn't score well enough on his tests, he won't get those specialties. What we need most are riflemen."

A snort from Fidel. "Dios mío, vieja. It's the Army. Of course he might go to war. That's why they call them soldiers."

Soledad ignored him. She turned to Bert. "Sign up for . . . este . . . cómo se dice, specioltos."

"You mean specialty, Mom," Gabby said, translating for his Mom as usual.

"Eso," she said.

"I don't know, Mom. I know how to work on cars already. And you know I'm not the smartest guy around. I don't think I could learn electronics. I sure don't type, so that's out. But I do know how to shoot a rifle."

"Mijo," Soledad implored.

"Ya basta," said Fidel. "The boy knows what he wants to do. If his fiancée doesn't mind, you shouldn't."

A warning look from Bert kept Angie from joining in.

"Mom, I'll be OK. And just because I join doesn't mean I'm going to Vietnam. Right, Sergeant?"

"Well, sorta," Benny said. "If you sign up as a rifleman, the chances get better that you'll go. But the other thing you need to remember, señora," turning to Soledad, "is that just because you go, doesn't mean you get hurt. I've done two tours in rifle companies and I'm here." He averted his eyes, not wanting to tell her of the wound that brought him home that second time.

"You see, Soledad. You shouldn't believe everything you see on television," Fidel said.

Soledad had not missed the CBS Evening News with Walter Cronkite since Bert announced he was going to join the Army. It seemed to Soledad that the United States was fighting two wars—one in Vietnam and another with people here who insisted that the war was wrong. Soledad didn't always follow the political arguments. She knew of Fidel's, Bert's, and Gabby's innate patriotism, but she thought it more machismo than patriotism.

"Mamá," Bert said, using the word guaranteed to soften Soledad. Usually, he called her "Mom." When he wanted something, it was "Mamá." It usually worked, too. Soledad missed the days when it was always Mamá. Even Gabby, following Bert's example, had not called her Mamá for a long time.

"Umberto," that's what she called Bert when she wanted to be stern, "We're not talking about BB guns." Yes, she knew about the BB gun wars.

She turned to Fidel. "The pictures don't lie," she said. Television and *The San Bernardino Evening Telegram* were full of war pictures. They weren't pretty.

"Soledad, he doesn't need our permission. He's a man."

"He's my hijo," Soledad said simply.

Benny didn't know what to say to that.

"Mamá, I'll be OK. Really. And Dad's right, I just want you to understand."

Benny saw his opening. "Let me tell you what happens after he joins."

He explained about boot camp—about rigorous training that builds strength and character. It also teaches you how to stay alive, though he said that more diplomatically. He spoke of other training opportunities. He discussed the GI bill and how Bert, after he completed service, would be able to go to college or buy a house on a VA loan.

Soledad knew it was a losing battle, but, her eyes brimming with tears, she made one last plea. "You'll have to promise," she said quietly.

"Excuse me," Benny said.

"You'll have to promise me that nothing will happen to Bert."

Benny should have told her he couldn't do that. He should have told her that there are no guarantees. Instead, against all common sense, he looked into her eyes and said, "I'll try to keep him safe." Soledad could tell that he meant it.

Tía Simona was still watering when Sergeant Benny climbed into his car. She regretted that it wasn't morning already, when she could walk over and hear all about the visit over pan dulce and café.

A Hot Summer: June 1968

Sergeant Benny couldn't get her out of his mind.

When he slept, he saw Soledad's smile. As he worked, he remembered her soft voice and her deep brown eyes.

Soledad thought of him too. She remembered the promise he made to keep Bert safe. She remembered his kindness, all the more appealing because it came from such an unlikely source.

Benny never doubted that he would see her again.

But the phone call surprised them both: Soledad when she dialed it, Benny when he answered it.

"Staff Sergeant Sánchez, United States Army recruiting station, San Bernardino. May I help you?" Benny snapped out in rote staccato.

"Buenos días," she said shyly, tentatively.

"Mrs. Rivera?"

And so it started.

Soledad said she wanted to know more about the Army.

Benny suggested a restaurant near the recruiting station.

There were awkward silences during Benny's rehearsed patter about the Army and its virtues. Soledad, in a print dress and unaccustomed stockings, rarely looked directly into Benny's eyes. When she did, Benny felt like his heart would burst.

"I want your promise. I want you to say it again," she said finally. "Bert is going to come back."

Benny told her the chances of a recruit going to Vietnam were generally slim. It depended on his MOS, his job specialty, and the needs in the field. Although he didn't mention this to Soledad, Benny was beginning to understand that being Mexican and an infantryman were both pretty strong indications you were going to Vietnam. Instead he told her that even if someone were sent to Vietnam, they were most likely to cool their heels in a rear support area.

He didn't go into detail about those rear areas, but Soledad sensed his derision. Benny was thinking how removed those rear areas were from the real war. Out in the boonies there was mortar fire, helicopter landings, and morose and frightened villagers. There was gunfire that came from nowhere and soldiers' eyes dulled from too much fear or too much mota—marijuana.

No, he couldn't tell Soledad about the rear areas where the favorite pastime was drinking and slapping flesh with hookers who seemed to rival the soldiers in vulgarity. Benny actually preferred combat.

"I want your promise," she repeated. "Bert is going to come back."

Benny could have told her—again—about the Army training, but he said simply, "I promise," and vowed to himself that he would do what he could to keep the vow.

Soledad peered into Benny's eyes and believed. Both smiled.

"Call me Soledad," she said, casting her eyes downward again.

"I'll call you Sally," he said suddenly.

Then the talk was no longer of the Army, Bert, or Vietnam. She had his promise. Instead they began the gentle spoken probing of lovers who did not yet know they were lovers. They talked of past lives, present travail, and yearnings.

Other lunches followed. Benny soon knew all about the entire family. He even knew how Fidel would come home quickly to shower, leaving again to be with his mistress.

He knew, without hearing, the whir-whirring of the old treadle Singer as Soledad did her morning sewing. He even knew Tía Simona had a hunchback. He vaguely remembered a neighbor fitting her description who was watering her lawn when he first visited the Riveras.

From lunches they progressed to dinners, then to assignations at the sergeant's apartment. Even then, though both knew where they were headed, they just talked.

She called him "Sargento." He was her new friend and confidant. She could tell him everything. She timed her meetings with Fidel's now almost nightly absences. She was always home before him, and Gabby, though confused by the comings and goings, was not going to complicate matters by saying anything. Nor was Bert.

"Do you want A-1 with your steak, Sally?" Benny asked as he set the table in his apartment.

A man doing the cooking was something new to Soledad. It was all she could do to remain seated at the kitchen table while Benny tended to pots and flipped steaks.

"Gracias, no," Soledad answered, not quite sure what A-1 was.

"Have Bert and Angie set the date yet?" Benny asked as they prepared to eat their steaks. The food tasted different to Soledad, as if her taste buds had been born anew. She watched as Benny carefully cut his steak into pieces, put down his knife, put his fork in the other hand, and carefully chewed. At first Soledad searched in vain for the tortillas. There were none. There were buttered dinner rolls, something Soledad brought out only for Thanksgiving. There were other treats: broccoli, mashed potatoes, and salad.

Soledad liked it. She liked the newness of everything. Benny smiled when he caught her staring at him. She smiled back and turned her eyes to her steak.

They talked easily about everything. About how Gabby was doing in school, Benny's orders, tías and tíos, brothers and sisters, and other mundane things. This too was strange to Soledad, talking with a man who actually conversed instead of grunting something incomprehensible between beers, belches, and television shows.

As they sat on the couch, however, there was still one unspoken topic.

When both began to feel warm and comfortable with one another, when eyes met and talk stopped, it meant it was time for Soledad to say goodbye.

But tonight, Benny reached over and stroked Soledad's cheek and said, "Sally."

And Soledad stayed.

"No," she whispered, but he continued stroking her cheek. She didn't resist when he pulled her to him.

The kiss was so unlike Fidel's quick and infrequent pecks.

It was long, soft, and lingering. She liked the scratch of Benny's beard as she caressed his cheeks.

Soledad didn't remember putting her arms around him, but she was very much aware of one of his hands as it started an unhurried journey from her knee, up her leg, over her hip, flirtingly close to her breast and around back, where it rested, moved, rested, and moved.

Such tenderness, she thought, pulling back momentarily and then returning to his embrace.

As he held her close, Benny felt her softness against his chest, her one hand caressing the back of his neck, the other around his waist. Their lips met, opened. Benny's tongue lovingly flicked and plunged hungrily. He nibbled her lips. She nibbled his, trying to learn.

It was all new to Soledad.

"Sally," he whispered again as he shifted position and gently pushed her back on the couch. Her arms came up under his arms and she clung to his chest.

Now his free hand roamed deliciously. No one had ever touched her like that.

Soledad didn't know what to do with her hands. Her legs parted naturally as his hand gently worked its way up her skirt, caressing her inner thighs and moving inexorably, teasingly, toward the increasingly wet spot. As his fingers slipped under the elastic and touched matted hair, she sighed, whispered once again, "No," more weakly this time, and her legs continued to part as a finger gently entered her lips.

Soon her hips were moving as the finger found the tiny button Fidel's fingers never knew existed.

His finger caressed the button, then wetted itself with her inner moisture, then stroked again. Benny's lips were first on her neck, then on her lips as Soledad tried to catch her breath.

Benny's finger touched here, then there, and her hips quickened their movement. A fleeting moment of panic seized Soledad as she realized she was out of control. She had never had these feelings.

"Dios. Dios," she whispered.

Soledad buried her lips against Benny's neck to muffle her cry. Her body shook, wracked by intense shudders of pleasure. She clung to Benny. So, that's what one feels like, she thought.

Benny sat up. Soledad looked into his eyes, smiled wanly, and then turned her face into the cushion.

"No," he said gently, taking her face into his hands and turning it toward him. "There is no shame between us. There is nothing but love."

He stood up and Soledad slowly pressed her skirt down, their eyes meeting again.

He took her hand and led her into the bedroom.

And there, on Sargento's bed, Soledad—who now cared not a whit that her nalgas were starting to sag or that her breasts were not as firm as they once were—took her new friend inside her and felt the pleasure again as he added his wetness to hers.

August 1968: A Wedding

Events were moving fast for Bert. Graduation was over. Boot camp loomed. He quit his job at the market. The store manager, whose own son was MIA in Vietnam, got misty-eyed saying goodbye.

As Bert put on his tux, butterflies fluttered in his belly. The bachelor party at the Catholic War Veterans' hall the night before had been raucous and drunken. He thought of all the tíos, cousins, and Chancellor carnales who would be crudos—hungover—and looking for succor at the backyard reception later. He wondered why he wasn't feeling worse. If butterflies were all he had to contend with, he was in great shape.

Just imagine it's Angie's quinceañera again, Bert told himself.

In another couple of hours she would be Angie Rivera. They would both stand up at the altar at St. Anthony's, where together they had received their First Holy Communion and Holy Confirmation, and become man and wife.

He thought of his mother and father. He didn't really know what was going on. He knew his father had a mistress, his mother was gone many evenings, and that the conversation was not too lively in the house these days. But he had had little time to reflect upon the changed atmosphere. He had been busy helping Angie with wedding plans and preparing to ship out to boot camp. He had even invited his recruiter, Sergeant Benny, to the wedding.

"Who ever heard of gray tuxes," Gabby whined.

"You want to be my best man or what?" Bert shot back.

Gabby struggled with his cummerbund. "Who ever heard of a twelve-year-old best man?" Gabby whined again. "And if I'm the best man, how come I didn't get to go to the bachelor's party?"

"OK, you can be my best boy. You got the ring?" Bert asked for the hundredth time.

Soledad thrust her head into the boys' room. "Apúrate. Hurry or you'll be late for your own wedding. Angie's almost ready." She saw Gabby wrestling with the cummerbund, slapped his hands away, and fastened it for him.

"Is Pop coming to the wedding?" Gabby asked.

She grabbed his shoulders, jerked him toward her, and said sternly, "He's your father. No matter what happens, remember that. Remember that he loves you both."

She pulled a Kleenex out of her pocket, dabbed at her eyes, and walked out.

Gabby looked at Bert, who shrugged. "It'll work out, chamaco."

"Everyone is leaving," Gabby said sadly. "You're out of here. Pop is as good as gone. I think this is the last party for a long time." Gabby could measure his life by parties—birthdays, quinceañeras, anniversaries, graduations.

Bert sat down on the bed. "I know it's hard. I feel good and bad all at the same time. But think of it this way. You're going to have the room all to yourself. No more oldies, and you can keep these too," he said, sticking his hand between Gabby's mattresses to pull out a *Playboy* centerfold.

The two laughed.

"How long have you known?"

"Sheeit, you think I don't know where those stains on my magazines come from. And speaking of stains, what are those things on the ceiling over your bed?" he said.

In the living room, Soledad thought the laughter sounded good. It had been a trying couple of months. Fidel and Dolores were now an open secret. Tía Simona commiserated daily, reciting a list of philanderers in the Rivera line. There was Fidel Sr., any number of his brothers, and—this surprised Soledad—Simona's own sainted husband, though he was a Rivera only by marriage.

"Sabes, it's part our fault," Simona said, her hunchback pushing her forward in the chair as she dipped her pan dulce. "Things have to change with us women so that they know we won't stand for it. That's how I ended my man's screwing around. I let him pick up his own calzones for a week, let him eat his own cooking, and took Enrique to my sister's house. He straightened up. Sabes, they leave their mamás who treat them like their caca is gold. We marry them and they get new mamás, except we sleep with them."

"Maybe the gringas and negras got it right: divorce," she said in hushed tones, looking around as if someone else might be listening in her own kitchen. "I don't know," she continued, shaking her head. "We can burn in hell down there or suffer right here."

Still, Soledad kept her relationship with the sergeant a secret. Thinking of Benny opened another wound. He would be leaving soon. He said his orders were due any day. Soon she would have only Gabby.

The drive to the church with Fidel and Gabby was quiet and tense. The caravan of shiny Chancellor cars, draped with white paper flowers, was already stretched in front of the church. Bert's orange Chevy, never shinier, was in the lead.

Fidel was miserable. He was crudo, hung over. Dolores was pressuring him for a commitment. Gabby was sullen and speaking to him only in monosyllables, and Soledad hardly spoke to him at all.

Fidel took his place at the back of the church, where he waited to usher guests to their pews. Around the church interior, light filtered in through the stations of the cross on stained glass.

Though Fidel was never a regular visitor to the church, he felt at home here. It was good that Bert was being married here, the same church he was married in. He stopped to say hello to the Army sergeant, who was already seated. "Early, aren't you, Sergeant?" he said.

Benny nearly jumped out of his uniform. "Wanted to get a good seat." Actually, he would use any excuse to be near Soledad.

Soledad saw Sargento sitting in the church. They had talked about whether he should come and had decided he should. Soledad always liked seeing him, though it would be difficult seeing but not touching him.

Soledad turned her eyes back toward the altar. She shot Gabby a look of admonishment to quit fidgeting as he stood next to Bert. She had never seen Bert look more nervous. Bert elbowed Gabby lightly. God, how he hoped Gabby had remembered to give the rings to the ring bearer.

Outside on the church steps, Angie prepared to walk down the aisle with her father. In front of her was a long line, with Petra, the maid of honor, at the head, followed by small cousins bearing flowers and rings and violet-gowned bridesmaids and their Chancellor escorts, all longtime friends of Bert and Angie.

Fidel joined Soledad in the pew. He really looked good in his blue suit, the only one he owned, Soledad admitted.

The music started and Bert's new life began.

Father O'Leary was relatively sober.

Soledad had confessed her affair to the Father, who counseled that she quit, forgive, and understand. He had to give the same counsel every week, however, because Soledad was not quitting until she had to and definitely was not forgiving or understanding. Penance was very long and hard on the knees, but Soledad considered it just part of the price she had to pay. In the corner candles burned, some of them lit by Tía Simona on Soledad's behalf.

The ceremony went smoothly, even if Bert did stutter out the "I do," and both Petra and Soledad had to shoot piercing looks at Gabby to quiet his giggles. Soledad started crying and tensed visibly when Fidel draped what was supposed to be a comforting arm around her shoulders.

After Gabby had paid the priest with money Fidel had given him, the procession left the church, and as the crowd began to spill out of the pews, Soledad and Sargento locked gazes. She smiled. Fidel wondered who she was smiling at.

She wished Benny could come to the reception.

Outside the church, rice rained down as Bert and Angie, her white train trailing, jumped into the orange Chevy. Horns were already starting to honk noisily and cameras flashed. With the door closed, Angie cried for joy.

The procession motored noisily away, flowers fluttering, Chancellor insignia bouncing at the back of each car. A few cars jolted up and down, hydraulics turning some high riders into low riders.

It was a royal wedding, Verdugo style.

Later in the Rivera backyard, Chancellors loosened their ties and took turns patrolling the perimeters for party-crashing Lords or other unwelcome guests. But there was little danger of that. Bert had asked Chuchi to be a sort of unofficial sergeant-at-arms. Police cars patrolled nervously. Too many family parties in this neighborhood ended in fights or worse.

Earlier, Tío Chuy had delivered the steer, roasted in his backyard pit. He also brought along goat, roasted the same way. Women ladled frijoles y arroz, and children, whose Sunday clothes bore no hint of the correct ladies and gentlemen of the wedding, chased one another through the yard and neighborhood.

It was a close-knit neighborhood and no one was likely to complain about the mariachi music, even after the sun had long set and the air cooled. Most the of the neighbors were at the party anyway.

Inside, Gabby was trying his best to look debonair, his tie

loosened, his jacket unbuttoned, and his hands thrust into his pockets.

Fidel ambled by drunkenly every once in a while to sniff the glass Gabby was holding.

Chuchi, khaki pants pressed for the occasion and wearing a shirt with buttons for once, held up the wall with Gabby. "Why's your dad come sniff your glass all the time?" he asked.

"Bert used to sneak drinks at family parties when he was my age. He got drunk once at my cousin Carmen's wedding and threw up. Mom was pissed. You drink?"

"Sometimes. It's kinda expected when you're a Lord."

"You think I should be a Lord sometime?"

"Only if you want me to kick your butt," Chuchi said softly.

"Then why do you do it?"

Chuchi thought about it. "Just a place to belong, I guess. The rucas too, I guess."

"Have you had one?" Gabby asked as if the question held no importance.

"Hell. One? You?"

"Yeah, sure. Plenty times," Gabby said.

They looked at one another and burst out laughing.

Louie came by to see if they were laughing at him.

"Hey, vatos. You look a-toda-madre in your tux, Gabby."

"It's how he gets all his women," Chuchi said, causing Gabby to gag and laugh at the same time.

Fidel came by and slapped Gabby on the back. "You drinking, boy?" he asked before returning to the keg.

In the kitchen Chuy's wife—the one he left his first wife for—was holding a baby on her hip and telling Soledad how she would make Chuy's life miserable if he ever went out with another woman.

God, Soledad thought, did everyone know about Fidel?

Yes, they did, Chuy's wife told her.

"And what do they think I should do?" she asked.

"The men say you should just wait until Fidel wakes up. They say he's a good man deep down," she said. "Come to think of it, that's what the women say too."

"And what would the men do if their wives took lovers?" Soledad asked.

Silence. "Leave, I guess. I mean, what else could they do?"

Later, after the guests had left and the women had cleaned up the mess, Soledad listened to the snoring coming from the bedroom. She went to the door, walked in, turned on the light, and shook Fidel awake.

"I want you out of this house in the morning. You go or I take Gabby with me to live in the streets. I won't shame myself or let you shame me anymore."

He was gone the next morning.

September 1968:
Orders and a Letter

He'd been waiting for several weeks, but he hesitated before opening the official document that would tell his future in very official terms.

Benny's orders had arrived.

He had requested another Vietnam tour, but that was months ago—before Soledad. She posed a problem. She was both a reason to stay and a reason to leave.

He had never considered himself a particularly moral person. He had, after all, actually killed people in the name of . . . Well, he wasn't precisely sure, but license and sanction had been given.

Soledad was married.

Yes, the marriage was on the rocks, but she was still married.

Benny took the letter opener, slipped it into the slot, and ripped upward.

He unfolded the paper. Fort Ord for a time and then Vietnam. He asked for it and the Army knew a sucker when they saw one. They also knew that experienced noncoms were a valued commodity in the war.

Benny looked up. Petty Officer Kozinski was standing in the doorway.

"Got what you wanted? Where you going?"

"Yea, I got what I wanted. Going to Nam. Going to camp for a while at Fort Ord until a slot opens up in a rifle company. The way the war's going, that won't be long."

"I don't know whether to say congratulations or what," the Navy man said. "I know I joke, but sitting on a tin can off the coast ain't exactly like what you guys do in-country."

Benny looked out the window. "A few weeks ago, I would have wanted the congratulations. Now, I don't know. I go where I'm told, go where I'm needed. If I wanted an easy job, I would have joined the pinchi Coast Guard."

The two men laughed. As much fun as they poked at each other's military branch, they shared the same opinion of the Coast Guard.

Well, he had made a promise to Soledad. Bert was also going to Fort Ord for basic training. The boy had not signed up for any MOS, though the testing he would undergo in boot camp might earmark him for some higher calling. But, in all likelihood, Bert was going to be a rifleman, and they aren't much good anywhere except where rifles are needed.

At home, Soledad busied herself packing for Bert, who would be leaving soon. They had told Bert not to pack much because they would give him all he needed in boot camp, but Soledad reasoned that he would still need calzones, some socks, his Bible, some pictures of his family, and a letter.

The letter told Bert how much she loved him, how much she would miss him, how she would pray every day and light a candle for him every Sunday. She wrote, in her halting English and scribbled Spanish, that he must take care of himself. She wrote it all because she could not say it without breaking down and crying.

Bert and Angie had been living with the Riveras since their marriage a month before. Soledad knew they did so mostly to look after her since Fidel had left. When Bert shipped off, Angie would go live with her folks and rejoin Bert if his orders took him to some post in this country, as she hoped.

Gabby had been sleeping on the couch.

"Querido hijo," Soledad wrote. "Yo sé que tú sabes things no están buenos entre your daddy and me. Yo pienso que you need to saber por qué.

"You're a man now. You have a wife muy buena, bonita y

cariñosa. You're lucky. Y espero que you will forever be happy together.

"Pero, things don't always work out entre husbands and wives. Your papá is a good man and I never want you to forget that. I won't say bad things about him. Pero necesito decirte que he forgot sometimes that he had a family that loved him. Or, tal vez, he knew we loved him y pensaba that he could do anything without losing that love.

"Es muy difícil decirte. Your daddy and I will not be getting back together. I will divorce your daddy. I have the papers from the lawyer. Quería esperar until you left. You've been so happy and that has made me happy too. I don't want that you hear it later from someone else. I know your tíos and tías will not be happy.

"Recuerda a tu familia. We will remember you in our thoughts and in our prayers. Por favor forgive me. El Padre O'Leary won't like it. Tal vez, El Señor tampoco.

"I worry that Gabby will be hurt and that he won't have you to talk to. Por favor, write him letters and tell him his mamá isn't a bad woman. Tell him that his daddy isn't a bad man. Tell him. Pues, tú sabes.

"Y recuerda that a mother always loves her hijo even if the love between a husband and wife todo el tiempo no es por vida. Pero, I know you and Angie will always be maridos and amantes. Que Dios te bendiga,

Tu madre."

And then she cried.

October 14, 1968:
Boot Camp

Boot camp was not like he imagined.

There was always some vato in your face. It wasn't like home. These guys could insult you all they wanted and you couldn't do a thing about it.

You did your marching, took your weapons instruction, and learned to not be yourself. Even Bert knew that everything in boot camp was designed to make soldiers bury their identities and start thinking as a team. There was no room for individuality here.

He missed Angie. He missed Mom, Pop, and Gabby.

But he *really* missed Angie. The weeks before boot camp were heaven. They balled their brains out. And they weren't always as careful as they should have been, though they both agreed this wasn't the best time for Angie to get pregnant.

He'd be surprised if she wasn't already pregnant, and the thought made him feel good. God, he missed her. He understood some of the muffled sniffling in the barracks at night. Others were having second thoughts too.

The others in the recruit company had similar stories. Some with high-school educations, more without. Mostly brown or black, with a good passel of poor whites thrown in. There were even a couple of college boys—or as Sergeant Olivos liked to say, "Big men on campus, but you ain't shit here." They had let their 2S draft deferments lapse by partying too much and flunking out of college.

Boot camp was a great equalizer. Every man among them, no matter what they said before they were drafted or enlisted, now insisted he wanted to go to Vietnam. Bert hadn't been much of a smoker before. He now smoked every chance he got. So did most of the other recruits. Bert didn't curse much before. He did now, as did everyone else. It was expected.

This was one big melting pot of testosterone and one-upmachoship—the glue that bonds males.

"Dear Mom:

"I read your letter. I wasn't surprised. I knew it was coming. I guess I was so happy, being with Angie and all, that I could kind of block it out. I will write a letter to the mocoso.

"Boot camp is hard. I miss all the familia. Don't tell Pete, but I miss her too. Ha Ha.

"It turns out the sergeant I signed up with got transferred here too. He came to see me. We're not supposed to have visitors but he arranged it somehow. I think he knows Sergeant Olivos, our drill instructor. He is a real tough vato. He's got this scar across his forehead. He told us that's where he took a mortar round but that he was too mean to die. Sergeant Benny told me though that he got it in a knife fight over a woman in Saigon or something like that.

"Anyway, it was nice of Sergeant Benny to come see me. He says he's going to Vietnam soon, as soon as a position in a rifle company comes open.

"We finished our testing yesterday. That's where we see what our MOS will be. MOS is that job specialty we were talking about. I don't think I did so good. Sorry. I think maybe I should have paid more attention in school. Let's just say I don't think they're going to make me a clerk or anything like that. And that's OK with me.

"I'm doing real good in other things though. I'm real good on the rifle range. I guess all those BB gun wars did some good. I'm also doing good at hand-to-hand. I'm recruit company corporal. That means I'm a squad leader in my company. I've got some neat guys in my squad.

"Gil Real is probably the best friend I got here. He's from

Oxnard and drives a '55. He got his girlfriend pregnant so he had to join. I want you to meet him. Maybe you will if you come to my graduation in ten weeks. It seems like forever.

"Another good friend I've made is Booker T. Jackson. We all call him Book. He's a negrito from Oakland. I guess I like them so much because we have so much in common. Gil was in a car club in Oxnard. His '55 is orange, like my Chevy. Book used to work in a store, too. He got drafted, though.

"We don't have much time to hang out together but we look out for each other. It's almost like having my Chancellor carnales with me, watching my back.

"They call reveille at 5:30 A.M., and in the morning we have to be out on the parade ground at 6 A.M. to march to breakfast. It seems like we drill all day. That's marching. When we're not drilling, we're on the rifle range or exercising or going through obstacle courses or having inspections or going to classes. It never stops. By the end of the day, we're all really tired.

"The food is real bad. The papas are mashed all the time. And the rice. It's white all the time. I never had white rice before. It has no taste. I like your arroz better. There's meat every day for every meal but sometimes you have to guess what it is. Like there is something here everybody calls caca on a shingle. It's meat and gravy on a piece of bread. It's horrible. They make you eat it all too. I can't wait to get home so you can cook me some carnitas, chicken mole, and menudo. I hope Angie gets to be as good a cook as you. As bad as the food is though, I'm gaining weight. I weigh 145 now but with all the marching it seems like it's all muscle. A week ago I could hardly walk from all the blisters on my feet, but they're hard now and my feet don't hurt no more.

"About Sergeant Benny. We talked a long time and he told me some good things about how to make things easier here for me. He taught me tricks for shining my boots and how to arrange my locker so it passes inspection. I'm teaching it to all the guys in my squad. We get the highest marks so far. Mostly he told me that I shouldn't take anything personal here. He said Sergeant Olivos is being a baboso on purpose because that's what drill sergeants are supposed to do. He told me that the sergeant is really a pretty good guy and a really good soldier. He's done two tours in Vietnam.

"I don't want to worry you, but I want you to start getting used to the idea. Sergeant Benny told me that I will probably be going to Vietnam too. I told him about my tests. After boot camp, I'll probably be going to advanced infantry training here at Fort Ord and then to Vietnam. I hope I get in his rifle company. I like him. I'm glad he came to see me, but I don't know why. Anyway, I got to go. It's almost 8 P.M. and that's lights out. Give my love to everyone. I will write Gabby and Pop. Don't worry. Everything will be all right.

"Love, Bert.

"P.S. Tell me if you need any money or anything, OK?"

Bert folded the letter and put it in the envelope. Taps played on a loudspeaker somewhere out in the night. "Lights out," went the call.

Bert plopped his head on the hard pillow and draped the scratchy green blanket over himself. A couple of bunks over, he could hear the creak-creaking of bed springs. He didn't know how some guys could jerk off in a room full of other guys, but they did.

"Hey, Duncan, that thing's going to fall off," someone sang out, followed by loud guffaws.

"Shut the fuck up," boomed another voice at the end of the barracks. That would be Sergeant Olivos doing his version of tucking the troops in. "If you guys got that much energy, maybe there's something we can do about that tomorrow."

Silence and then muffled sniffling.

How many more tomorrows until graduation? Bert thought as sleep took him.

He thought of going home in his uniform. His tíos would razz him about his haircut, but they would all be proud. He and Angie would cruise in his '58 for one final fling before he had to ship out again. He imagined the admiring stares at his uniform, the expert-marksmanship ribbon, and Angie.

Back home, Angie was thinking of Bert, too. She had missed her period. Somehow she knew it wasn't coming back for a while. "Damn you, Bert," she muttered as she watched *The Man from U.N.C.L.E.*, "I told you we should have used the rubber."

"¿Qué, qué, mija?" her mother said from the other chair. "Nothing, Mamá."

No one was going to believe she got pregnant in a month of marriage. So what? she thought. She wondered if she should move out if she had the baby and Bert was sent overseas, but she knew her parents would never stand for that.

God, I'm going to get fat, she thought, as Bert, a couple of hundred miles north, was smiling in his sleep.

October 23, 1968: Crudo en Verdugo

Pop and Bert were gone. Even Angie left to go back to her parents' home, though she still came by every day to see Mom. Gabby reacted as stoically as a twelve-year-old boy could. That meant he vented his frustration out of earshot of his mother and in ways she could not have imagined.

Fidel came to see Gabby on weekends, but the silence between them made the situation painful. Fidel didn't know how to explain, and Gabby didn't know how to ask. So they went to soccer games and movies or to get burgers or burritos. In truth, Gabby was seeing more of his pop than he ever had.

"C'mon, Chuchi. You can take us to the beer bust," Louie was pestering.

The three sat in front of Gabby's house. The sight of a Royal Lord wearing colors sitting on her front lawn didn't make Soledad feel very good as she looked out the window. Next door, Tía Simona was making mental notes on what she would tell Soledad about the pachuco.

"You guys are a little young. You want to go, Gabby?" Chuchi asked.

"I don't know," Gabby said, glumly.

Chuchi knew what was bugging Gabby. All of 14th Street knew. Still, it wasn't something they would talk about.

"If you go, you guys don't drink and you don't act like pendejos."

Tía Simona watched as the trio walked past her house. Chuchi was going to come to no good, she thought. His mother is a puta who doesn't know who the fathers are of half her children. It's not good that Gabby spends so much time with him. She'd talk with Soledad. She'd also talk to Louie's mom. Gabby saw her hunchbacked figure looming in the window and knew he'd hear about it later.

Who gives a shit, he thought.

The trio walked to a house with music blaring from the backyard, where an 8-track stereo was jerry-rigged to a car battery. Gabby wondered which of the neighbors wouldn't be able to start his car.

A silver keg commanded all the attention, manned by a fattish vato, white T-shirt draped over a beer belly and a hairnet holding down slicked-back hair. He pumped the keg, trying to coax more than foam through the tube.

"C'mon, ése," said a skinny Lord.

He tried again and some golden liquid flowed from the spout at the end of the clear tube. "Órale," he said, as he started filling plastic cups.

Many of the Lords were already in various stages of drunkenness. No one put up much of a fuss at the arrival of Gabby and Louie, but that had more to do with the company they were keeping.

"Hey, Chuchi ése," said the Lords, exchanging intricate handshakes.

A couple of old couches and car seats constituted the lawn furniture, along with some wooden boxes.

Those Lords who had rucas sat next to them, draped arms and hickeys signifying ownership.

Other Lords crouched vato style, elbows resting on laps and backs hunched.

Gabby and Louie staked out a corner and struck similar poses.

"You going to get any beer?" asked Louie.

"I don't know," said Gabby.

"C'mon," pleaded Louie. "I'll do it if you do."

"Don't be stupid. We at least got to wait until they're a

little drunker," Gabby said. That, at least, was how it worked at Pop's parties.

Chuchi was talking with a Lord named Johnny Soto, rail thin with bulging, tattooed arms.

"Who're the chamacos? That one's Bert Rivera's little brother, ain't he?"

"Yea, they're good guys."

"I hear Bert went airborne."

"Nah, just a grunt. He's in boot camp right now. Gabby's having it rough right now. His pop left too," Chuchi said.

Both nodded, neither a stranger to dysfunctional family life. The Lords made their own family.

"Maybe they want to be Junior Lords." The Junior Lords were Royal Lord wannabes.

"I don't think so. They're civilians. Gabby's pretty good in school. Let's leave them alone. I just wanted them to come see we weren't as crazy as people think."

Johnny smiled, "But we are."

The 8-track blared the Temptations and two couples got up to dance.

A group of Lords started poking fun at one of the dancers. He flipped them off and kept on dancing, a sort of shuffle, his shoulders swaying more than his feet moved.

A couple of rucas off by themselves were looking at Gabby and Louie, giggling. They bounced over to the boys, who were still striking the chuco pose.

"Let's dance," they said. Louie looked at Gabby wide-eyed, gulped, and nodded.

"You're Bert's brother, huh?" Loca asked as her wide hips swayed. Gabby nodded as he attempted the Temptation step.

A little ways off, a fumbling Louie was trying some unknown step, and his ruca was smiling.

"Is Angie pregnant?" Loca asked.

"Maybe. We don't know for sure yet."

Louie and Gabby caught the attention of the rest of the Lords, who cheered them on.

"Órale, vatos. Get down!"

"Hey, Loca. Getting them kinda young now."

She stuck out her tongue. "I like 'em cute and young so I can teach them to do it better than you do."

The Lords whooped and razzed the embarrassed heckler.

This is going to be a great day, Gabby thought.

Things got sort of fuzzy after that. Someone shoved a cup of beer in front of Gabby and he drank that, and another, and another. Pretty soon he was sitting next to Loca with her arm around him.

"I think I love you," Gabby slurred.

"You're so cute," she said and kissed him on the cheek.

"Gabby, you OK?" Chuchi was standing above him.

How did I get on the ground? Gabby thought.

"I think I'm going to be sick. Where's Loca? I think I love her, Chuchi. Oh, God, I'm drunk."

Chuchi shook his head. "I'll take care of you. Let's go."

Next thing, he was in a car jammed full of Lords.

"He better not get sick back there, Chuchi," the driver said.

"Shut up."

"Chuchi, Chuchi. Where's Loca?"

"I'm here, mijo."

God, "mijo" sounded better coming from her than from Mom.

"We're just cruising 'til you come down," Chuchi said.

"I'm going to be sick."

"Get him the fuck out of the car!" the driver shouted.

Then Chuchi was patting Gabby on the back. Gabby was on all fours. He was staring down at a puddle. Where did that come from?

"I'm OK. I'm OK. I'm soooo drunk." Gabby was having a good time.

"Gabby, you OK?" That was Louie. How come he wasn't drunk?

"Don't get used to it, ése. It's the last time you go to a beer bust," said Chuchi.

"Leave him alone. He's cute." That was sweet Loca, Gabby thought, but wasn't quite sure.

Gabby wondered if he had made love to her yet. God, he thought, wouldn't it be sad if he had and couldn't remember. He lost his cherry and couldn't even remember. He felt like crying. "Did I lose my cherry, Chuchi?"

Laughter. "Not yet, mijo. Give yourself a couple of years," Loca said.

Then everything went dark again.

When he regained consciousness, he was in Chuchi's backyard.

"Don't bring that boy into my house," a woman was shouting.

He could hear Louie and Chuchi talking. "How are we going to get him home, man?" Louie was asking.

"He's going to have to spend the night here. You too or else they'll get the truth out of you. You'll have to call his mom and yours. You'll be in trouble tomorrow, but not as much as if you went home drunk tonight."

Chuchi's was the voice of experience.

Gabby fell asleep on whatever he was lying on. God, this was a great night. He'd worry about tomorrow, tomorrow.

December 1968

In splendid green uniform, buffed with muscles that hadn't been there before, Bert walked through the back door to the kitchen.

"Ay, Dios mío," Soledad cried, dropping the bolita of masa for the tortilla she was about to flatten and flip on to the comal.

"Is that for me?" Bert asked, pointing at the masa on the floor.

"Tonto. Angie said you'd be coming home tomorrow. Ay, Dios mío, nothing's ready." It wasn't really a scolding. Angie walked in behind him, smiling broadly.

"Gabby, Gabby! Your brother's home!" Soledad shouted.

Gabby barreled through the hallway, crashing into Bert.

Pop wasn't around, but Bert expected that. Later, he would stop by to see his dad at the "puta's" house. That's what Angie said Soledad and Tía Simona called Dolores. Bert wasn't precisely looking forward to it.

Soledad wiped her face with a dish rag. "There's nothing to eat. You should have *tole* me you were coming."

"Mom. Mom. It's OK. I'm taking you guys out to dinner."

Boot camp had been hell. The marching and drilling weren't so bad, but he had been so homesick. Often, he curled up like a fetus under the scratchy green army blankets—he missed Angie so much. But he hung with it. And when Angie watched him march on parade during graduation at Fort Ord, he was so proud.

Angie had cried.

Earlier, when she wrote him that she was pregnant, he let loose a grito and cried with joy. "We're going to have a baby. We're going to have a baby," he babbled. Gil Real, whose own girlfriend—now wife—was pregnant, understood.

Angie wasn't showing yet, but then boot camp was only twelve weeks long. She would be by the time he finished advanced infantry training.

God, it seemed so long since he lived here. It was hard to believe that he'd been gone for only three months. The trek down the hallway, where all the family pictures hung, almost made him cry. Soledad hadn't taken down the photos of Pop.

On its battered table, the old black and white set looked obsolete to Bert now. The furniture looked a little more worn than he remembered, the Tijuana blanket over the couch looked more tacky. There was the Hamm's Beer sign. He'd turn on the waterfall later for old time's sake. And it all looked so good. It seemed like even Gabby had changed. Not quite the mocoso he had left—a bit taller and a bit harder. Certainly not as talkative.

It was plain Gabby was impressed by the uniform and the lean look of the returning hero.

"Are you going to Vietnam?" Gabby asked.

Soledad winced.

"Looks like," Bert said simply. "Let's change the subject."

Bert tried to take them out to a restaurant, but Soledad wouldn't hear of it.

"Look at you. You're so skinny. Just take me to the store."

It felt good listening to Angie and Soledad make a racket in the kitchen, pots clanging, meat sizzling, and chatter interrupted periodically by laughter. Pedo was torn between wanting to investigate the aroma floating from the kitchen and shaking his butt in front of Bert.

Later, over fried pork chunks with green chile, frijoles, arroz, and fresh homemade tortillas, Bert told them about boot camp.

"Nothing like this in boot camp," he said, taking a piece of tortilla to wipe the plate.

Bert found Gabby in the room they had once shared. He

was lying on the bed, eyes closed, listening to the "Duke of Earl."

"¿Qué pasó? You like my oldies after all."

"They're OK. Thanks for leaving them."

The room looked much different, younger. The stereo was in its usual place, but instead of posters of cars and photos of Angie, there were some model airplanes on the shelf and a Temptations poster.

"How you getting along? How's Mom doing?"

"We're doing OK. Things are just different. I probably see Pop more now than ever. He takes me places on weekends. I've seen more movies in the last three months than I have in the last three years."

Soledad had asked Bert to talk to Gabby. Gabby thought his single bout with drunkenness had not been noticed. Not so. Soledad was worried. She liked Chuchi—actually felt sorry for him—but didn't know if she liked Gabby hanging out with him. The Lords jacket in the house always raised her hackles.

"Mom says you're letting your school work go a little bit. Don't you like junior high?" It was the same junior high Bert had attended.

"No, it's a-toda-madre," Gabby said. "It's just that it doesn't seem all that important anymore. It's harder, too."

Gabby remembered his initial confusion at having to go from one class to another instead of staying in one class-room with one teacher all day. But he got used to it. He still hung out with Louie and his other old friends. Still, it was different. He noticed girls more. He particularly noticed that they had filled out in the summer, no longer the skinny, pig-tailed girls of elementary school. He was having a hard time not getting a hard-on all the time. Someone should have explained the onset of puberty to him. When it happened, he walked with his notebook in front of his crotch. He noticed a lot of other chavalos did the same.

"Mom wants me to lecture you," Bert said, sitting on his old bed. "I guess she figures I was thirteen once too. And I remember going to Sturges for the first time and thinking I had to act all bad. I didn't have to, you know, but you couldn't have told me that then. She said you got drunk. Is that true?"

So she did know. "It was just once. Chuchi let us go to a beer bust. He told us not to drink, but Louie and I did anyway. He took care of us."

Bert nodded. He trusted Chuchi more than Soledad did.

"You're starting a little earlier than I did. You know, that stuff will fuck you up."

"I know. I was sicker than a dog the next day. I don't think it's going to happen *ever* again."

"Well, chavalo, it'll happen again. It's part of growing up around here. The thing you got to remember is that you can drink but not get drunk."

Gabby was grateful that Bert wasn't scolding him, but he had other things on his mind. "I'm worried about Mom. I can't tell if she misses Pop or not. And money is kinda tight. Pop, I think, still makes the house payment. I think Mom's lawyer is making him do that. But he really doesn't want to pay anything else. He told me that he doesn't want to pay Mom to sleep with other men. I didn't say anything, but I don't think that's something he should have told me."

Soledad pulled in as much in sewing money as she could. She had applied for a seamstress job at Harris, a local department store, and had set up her own checking account The bills were getting paid. She surprised herself with her self-sufficiency.

Gabby tried to help out. He'd taken a morning paper route and this too, he thought, made him less attentive at school. He was very sleepy sometimes. He used the money to buy his own clothes, though he was still using some of Bert's hand-me-downs.

"You changed your hair," Bert said.

Gabby's hair was slicked back, the pomade making it shine greasy black.

"What do you think?"

"It makes you look like you're trying to grow up too fast, but if you like it that's all that counts."

"At least I got some hair, vato."

They laughed as Bert ran his hand over his close-cropped cut. "It'll grow back."

Silence. The two sat on their beds, deep in their own thoughts.

"I want things to be the same they always were," Gabby said suddenly. "You left. Pop left. I think Mom has been seeing somebody else. There are letters she hides from me. She doesn't let me see her, but I think she cries sometimes. She doesn't want to talk about it. Sometimes I really hate Pop."

Bert didn't know how to make sense of this for Gabby. You go through life as a kid thinking how boring things are, then when the changes happen, you just want it the way it was. "Life is about changes, I think. They're not all good. My sergeant tells us, 'What doesn't kill you makes you stronger.' That might be bullshit, I don't know. But it sounds true. It feels true anyway after boot camp.

"I feel bad that I'm not here for you, mocoso, but I think you're going to do the right thing most of the time. I look at you and think what a baboso I was at your age. You're smarter than I was. You're sure growing up faster.

"But listen, don't hate Pop. I did at first, too. You know, really, we only know one side of this story. I guess Pop needed things we couldn't give him. Maybe that's his fault. Maybe that's ours."

Gabby thought about that. "I understand more than you think I do," Gabby said, turning red. "It seems like I got a huesón all the time now."

Bert laughed but regretted it when he saw Gabby's face.

He apologized and tried to explain that hard-ons were all part of life at thirteen.

"No, what I mean is that I know about wanting to get laid," Gabby said. "Sometimes I want it more than anything in the world. And I see you're not really like that, so I know I'm probably going to grow out of this all-the-time horniness. But I think Pop maybe never did. I think maybe Pop is more of a kid than I am sometimes.

"It's like how he used to tease us all the time. It was fun, but it was him being a kid. It seems like Mom was the only grown-up in the family, but she's the one we teased the most.

"I mean, you remember Pop getting angry? Man, I used to think I could act like a baby when I didn't get my way, but Pop beat me at that any day. He threw things and cussed, 'Cabrón this,' and 'Cabrona that.' And maybe it was just because we were out of beer or I turned the channel or something.

"I think if things ever do get back to normal, Pop's the one who has to grow up."

Bert and Gabby fell silent, and Bert wondered, "Who's more grown up, me or Gabby?"

1969: A New Year

Life developed into a routine for Fidel and Dolores.

Maybe this is what married life is like, Dolores thought. She had a man of her own coming home to her every night. She cooked for him. He'd eat and grunt his approval.

At first they made love every night with a vengeance. And truth was, Fidel was motivated in part by revenge. Then it became rote. Sometimes nothing worked at all.

She told him not to worry about it. Fidel's mind, she could tell, was elsewhere. She could see the guilt eating at him. Even as he lay with her, she could see his anger at the possibility that his wife might be with someone else. She imagined it would get better once he got past the hurt. Perhaps he would come around once she got pregnant.

"Ay, Papacito. Don't worry about it. It comes up eventually. You've just had a rough time lately," she said sympathetically.

Then one day Bert came to visit. It was awkward. Fidel introduced Dolores to him, but didn't quite know what kind of billing to give her.

"This is my, er, uh, friend," he said. He saw Dolores wince out of the corner of his eye.

After Bert left—he was in a hurry to leave, really—Dolores asked incredulously, "Your friend? Is that what I am? Your friend?"

"Give it a rest, woman. What was I supposed to say? This is the woman I left your mother for?"

"Your friend? Fidel, I'm your fiancée."

Fidel fell silent. "I don't remember asking you to marry me."

Dolores was stunned. She assumed, of course, that marriage was what the relationship was ultimately about. With one sentence, Fidel had destroyed plans and dreams—she had even taken to putting a pillow on her stomach below her dress to see how she would look when she got pregnant.

Sure, she wasn't wearing a ring, but she had assumed . . .

"Then what are we doing? Am I just your puta until you decide to go back to your wife?"

"Puta is your word. We're two people who are giving each other comfort. We like being together. Listen, I care for you, but I'm not even divorced yet and you're thinking marriage. I don't know if I'm going to be ready for that anytime soon. Let's just enjoy what we have, OK?"

"No, it's not OK. I want you to tell me right now what our plans are. Do you even love me?"

Never in their entire relationship had Fidel said so, she now remembered. But of course he did, she thought. I give him comfort. I lay with him. I cook for him. I'm trying to get pregnant for him.

"Let's not talk about it," Fidel said as he stalked to the kitchen to get a beer.

Dolores followed him. "We might as well get it out now. I asked you a question. Do you love me?"

Fidel sighed, feeling all of a sudden a beaten man. "I don't know," he said honestly. "I care for you but right now I'm a very mixed-up man who just lost his family. I don't know where we're going."

Sympathy softened Dolores's features.

"I know it's been hard, Papacito. I just have to know if we have a chance for a future. I'll wait if you want me to."

Maybe getting pregnant right now would not be such a good idea, she thought suddenly. She paused, thinking how to tackle this delicate issue. "But, Papacito, if we're going to wait, maybe you should start wearing those things."

Fidel looked puzzled.

"You know," she whispered. "Those rubber or plastic

things men put on their, their, things. Tú sabes, so I won't get pregnant before we're ready."

Fidel hadn't really thought about it. He hadn't had to. It should have been obvious to Dolores, he thought, that he was shooting blanks. But all Dolores knew was that he had fathered two children and that Soledad had miscarried a few times as well.

"We don't have to worry about that," he said.

"What do you mean? Yes, we do. Fidel, I don't want to end up pregnant and alone. I don't want to be pregnant while you make up your mind if you love me or not."

"That's not what I mean. I mean we don't have to worry about it because you can't get pregnant. I mean I can't make you pregnant."

Dolores's eyes narrowed then widened as understanding dawned. "You better not be saying what I think you're saying. You got yourself fixed? All this getting into bed has just been about you satisfying your urges? Please tell me you didn't get yourself fixed just so you can get between my legs without worrying about making babies." Dolores's face reddened. She looked around as if for something to throw.

"No, I didn't get myself fixed to keep from getting you pregnant. I got myself fixed after Gabby because Soledad had a rough time losing those babies before Gabby was born."

"You bastard! I'm not your first, am I? You've been going out on your wife long before you met me. I was just the one you were with when she caught you. That's why you're here. Not because you love me. Not because you want to marry me. Not because you want to have a family with me." She was crying now.

"I should have known. How stupid can I be. I'm such a fool. It all comes to me now. How could you ever trust a man who steps out on his wife. If he lies to her, he'll lie to anybody."

"Wait a goddamn minute, Dolores. I never lied to you.

When we first met, I could have told you I wasn't married. You knew. I never said I loved you or that I wanted to make babies with you. This has been good for both of us. We've both gotten a little of what we've needed."

"You don't understand a goddamn thing about what I need. I need a man. Not half a man. And that's what I'd be getting with you. A man who's lied to everybody he's loved and fooled me into thinking he loved me. A man who can't even make babies." Dolores sat on the bed and plunked her head into the pillow.

"Wait a minute. I never told you I loved you. I never told you I could make babies. You don't want a man. You want a baby maker."

Dolores raised her head from the pillow. "Whatever I want, it's not you. Get out. I said, get out!"

That's how it ended.

Fidel stayed a while with his brother Chuy. Chuy understood perfectly.

Chuy's new wife, however, didn't understand at all. In her mind, she was no longer the other woman but the married woman, the winner. She was on Soledad's side. Besides, she didn't want Fidel around to remind her of her own role in Chuy's infidelity or to remind Chuy that he was perfectly capable of stepping out on her too.

So Fidel, tired of the cold treatment, found his own apartment after a couple of weeks. It was better that way, he told himself. Now he could see anybody he wanted, anytime he wanted.

And, at first, he did. He hung out a lot at the Catholic Veterans' hall, picking up the barflies there, but waking up with a boozy, fat woman got old fast.

So Fidel started going to other bars. He let his hair grow. He wore his shirt open, a Virgen medal on a gold chain. He started wearing leisure suits.

But, though the women he brought home were not precisely barflies anymore, Fidel found he didn't like women who treated sexual liaisons as casually as he did. They didn't care if he didn't call again, and they never called him. One-night stands, Fidel thought, were not what they were cracked up to be. As freethinking as he thought he had become, the sexual revolution was not a good fit for him.

So he sat alone in his furnished studio apartment. He missed his Hamm's Beer sign. He would have to ask Soledad for that. She had balked at him putting it up anyway. Every weekend he saw Gabby, but most nights he watched television and drank beer.

And Dolores?

Henry was looking good.

March 1969

No one could have prepared Bert for Vietnam.

He feigned bravado for Angie before he left, for his Army partners during advanced training at Fort Ord, and again during further instructions at Schoefield Barracks in Hawaii, But in Vietnam he was just plain scared.

As Bert sat in the muddy puddle, mortars exploding around him, flares overhead, the staccato rat-a-tat-tat of automatic fire, he knew no amount of training could have possibly prepared him.

"Welcome to Vietnam," the banner had said at the steamy, hot military airbase where his C-130 had landed. He, Gil Real, Book Jackson, two others from boot camp, and fifteen others from advanced training were told to check their gear. They sweated in the oppressive tropical heat and waited.

Two hours later, Bert and the others were hunched down in Hueys going in-country. Down below, green jungle canopy and lush fields passed by. He made the sign of the cross, felt for La Virgen under his uniform, and looked expectantly at Sergeant Benny. Bert didn't know how Benny had swung it, but they belonged to the same outfit.

Later, in a hole in the ground, all Bert could feel was his own fear. Booker had been killed by mortar fire during the first half-hour, his body shielding Bert from the bursting shrapnel.

It wasn't supposed to be like this. "Oh, God, please don't make me have to move anywhere," he thought.

Sergeant Benny watched Bert and knew what he was feeling. He'd been there. He crawled over to Bert. "C'mon boy, snap out of it! It's not going to get any better."

"I can't do this! I can't do this!" Bert shouted over the din of battle.

"Goddamn it, boy. This is what we get paid for. You going to just sit here until the gooks get your range with their mortars? We got to move. Now! Look at me. Look into my eyes," the sergeant said, grabbing Bert by the shoulders.

Bert forced himself to look into the sergeant's face.

"Listen to me. I made Sally—I mean your mom—a promise. You're going to live through this. Do you hear me? Now, move!"

Bert got up on his knees, turned away, and threw up—deep, heaving retchings spilling everything from his guts.

He turned and looked at the sergeant. "OK, I'm ready," he said weakly.

"Attaboy. Let's go, you worthless vatos." And he, Bert, Gil, and six other survivors ran in jagged patterns out of the hole, through the open field, and toward the line where other soldiers were starting to rally and lay down a covering fire. Overhead, gunships roared and machine guns fired. Steady rifle and mortar fire poured from the dense jungle behind them.

"God," Bert said, clutching at La Virgen. His father had given the medallion to him before he left.

"This kept me safe in Korea, mijo," was all Fidel had said, unaccustomed tears in his eyes.

Bert ran like he'd never run before. On his left, Real shouted in pain and went down. Benny was there, trying to pick him up and not having much luck because of Real's convulsions.

Bert ran back. He took Real's left side and Sergeant Benny took the other. They ran another hundred or so yards. Some fellow grunts ran out to meet them. They had crosses on their helmets. They looked like angels to Bert. Together they wrestled Real into a hole where stretchers waited. Real was screaming, "I don't want to die. Please, Sergeant Benny, don't let me die." He looked at Bert, his eyes wide and scared. Then he died, eyes still open.

Bert looked at his arm where he had gripped his friend. It

was soaked with dark red, almost black, blood. Real had got it in the back. Bert looked around. The sergeant, himself, and four others were left from the original group.

He shot a puzzled look at Benny, who shook his head and said, "They didn't make it." Mancuso and Lake, two youths from advanced infantry training, were missing. Mancuso smoked Newports and had bad acne, Bert remembered. Lake was from Tucson. The medic crouching by Real shook his head, took off his dog tags, and waved for another body bag.

That was Bert's introduction to Vietnam. Of the twenty-one who made the trip from Fort Ord to Vietnam, just six remained. They had been in Vietnam four hours.

An officer told Bert they won the battle. Bert didn't know how that could be. But it was official: 127 "gooks" killed that day, the second lieutenant said proudly. Bert hadn't seen a single body other than those of his comrades. On the U.S. side, 49 killed, 27 wounded. A clear victory, the second lieutenant told Benny, Bert, and the other dazed survivors. They had helped, the lieutenant said.

It was supposed to make them feel good. It didn't. Gil's daughter had been born just a week before. He had been so happy. Bert had met Gil's wife at boot-camp graduation. She was going to take it hard.

Sergeant Benny told him later that someone screwed up. No way were raw recruits supposed to be sent in-country right away. But the battle raged, and someone needed bodies to throw at Charlie.

Three weeks and five firefights later, Sergeant Benny's squad pulled out with the rest of the regiment. Yes, a very clear victory, other higher ranking officers told them.

So why, Bert asked himself, weren't they staying on this piece of real estate Americans died for?

"Welcome to Vietnam," Sergeant Benny said as they boarded the chopper for a rear area. "All you got to know is that you're alive. You done good, boy."

Bert knew he had. He was alive. He had survived six firefights. He had looked down his sights at moving bodies and seen more than a few go down after he fired. He threw up again the first time he saw someone fall. BB-gun wars and shooting flies off dog turds had made him a good marksman, but this was no game.

He wrestled with death, literally, going hand-to-hand briefly with a youth in black pajamas, both scared and both wanting to live. Bert was thankful for the 14th-Street training. On 14th Street there was no such thing as dirty fighting. There were only winners and losers. He kicked, elbowed, and wrestled the other youth, until Benny cracked the Vietnamese boy's head open with the barrel of his M-16. Bert didn't know if he was dead, and he and the others didn't stay to find out.

That seemed ages ago.

Right now, he was on his way to a well-deserved drunk and feeling guilty. He was alive and others weren't. He had not written Angie a letter since Hawaii. He hadn't known what to write. He still didn't.

In the bar, soldiers in varying degrees of drunkenness yahooed along to shitkicker music. On the stage a pretty Vietnamese girl in cowboy boots gyrated in a striptease to a Merle Haggard tune.

Bert wasn't interested.

It was all so confusing. Why was he here?

A hand gripped his shoulder.

He looked around at Benny.

"C'mon boy, let's go find some better music."

They strolled into the night. It had been a small Vietnamese hamlet until the Army base went up next door. Now, every fourth building was a bar, every tenth, a whorehouse.

"You been laid yet?" Benny asked as they strolled back toward the base and the barracks.

Bert cast a sidelong glance at Benny to see if was kidding.

He was, though it was hard to tell from Benny's hardened features.

"Angie'd have my ass if I came home with the clap. No thanks."

Benny nodded. He felt the same way about Soledad, Sally.

They passed an alley and a sweet aroma wafted over from a group of men in hushed conversation, the glowing embers of reefers lighting the shadows.

"You want to stay away from pot around here. It's industrial strength and it'll fuck up your head," Benny said as they continued walking. "You done tried some already?"

Bert shook his head but knew that if he got any more scared, he'd be hitting the mota hard. He had seen some of the vets in the last three weeks smoke it just to keep from going crazy.

"The problem with that shit is that it don't let you think straight when you got to. More potheads getting it out there than anybody else. They think it makes them forget their fear, but that stuff makes you feel anything you're feeling a hundred times stronger. And then you just get stupid. The right amount of fear is what keeps us alive. Besides, they tell me they're lacing it with heroin."

Yeah, Bert had heard that too, along with the story about the incurable syphilis that makes your camote rot away. There's a Navy ship out there, just cruising, with all the incurable syphilis guys aboard just waiting for a cure. Or so the story went.

After they got past the gate, they heard more shitkicker music from barracks where the Southern, Midwestern, and Western boys gathered every night to drink beer.

Past another barrack and Motown blared, Aretha making her plea for respect. This was where the blacks gathered to do their secret, complicated handshakes that involved no actual gripping of hands at all, or so it seemed.

On to the enlisted men's club where this week a Filipino

band flown in special was playing a mixture of oldies and requests from the mostly Chicano crowd. "La Bamba" and "Volver, volver" played often this night.

Benny and Bert sat down and ordered. They didn't say much. They didn't need to. They were bonded now by battle and death. It didn't take "La Bamba" or the gritos aborning to tell them that.

Tomorrow Bert would write the letter.

April 1969

"Yes, it's true. The puta is after my Henry."

Tía Simona dipped the pan dulce into her coffee. Soledad and Angie merely picked at theirs. They were sitting in Soledad's kitchen.

"Mija, eat something. Please, you're eating for two," Simona told Angie.

Angie, in a maternity frock, looked down at her belly and smiled.

"It feels like twenty-two," she said.

"No, no. There are not that many cuates with the Riveras. Are there twins in your family? No? Well, like I was saying, after Fidel left Dolores, she's had her eyes on Henry."

Soledad knew that Fidel had left his mistress months earlier. Still, she had no intention of seeking Fidel out. She was missing Sergeant Benny too much.

But how and why her family life had disintegrated so suddenly was still a hot topic with her and the two she had grown especially close to since the breakup. Simona, though Fidel's aunt, had become a pillar of strength for her, and Angie stopped over often just to see how she was doing.

"How do you think men think?" Soledad asked pensively. "I mean, how can a man live with the woman who gives him his babies, cooks his food, and sleeps with him, and then want other women?"

She had asked herself that question a million times and had no answers. In her mind, she did not start her romance with Benny until Fidel had left, in spirit if not in body.

"It's maybe like my mother said," Simona offered. "Men are children. They want what they want when they want it. And they think they can have it all: strong sons and virtuous wives and daughters. And if you're too tired to make love sometimes or maybe it's not so exciting making love to the same man who farts and burps in front of you like you're not there, well, that's reason enough for him to go out and get what he wants when he wants it."

She dipped her bread into her coffee again, trying to calm herself.

Angie looked at both women and said, "Do you think Bert will ever be like that?"

"Pues, mija, it's just a thing they go through sometimes for some of them. For others, it's all the time. And for others, they got all they want at home," said Simona, splashing coffee on the table as she pointed with her pan dulce.

Soledad could see Angie wasn't reassured. "No, I don't think Bert is like that. I don't think you'd let him be," Soledad said.

Angie looked puzzled.

"I think it's like this: some of it is our fault. I married young and didn't know that anything I thought or anything I said mattered. I'm just a girl, I thought. That's what I learned at home. My mother picked up my father's calzones and my brothers' calzones. We girls washed dishes, cleaned house, and, when we were old enough, helped my mother pick up after my father and my brothers.

"Sabes, I don't remember my father ever asking my mother what she thought about anything. And when he wanted to go out, he was just like Fidel. 'Where you going, Papá?' 'Out,' he'd say, just like Fidel. And just like my mother, I'd not say anything."

"Not me," said Simona. "I always told my husband—Dios rest his soul—what was on my mind. Maybe too much. He had his little puta on the side until I told him what I thought about that. Then he quit."

"So, what are you saying?" Angie asked. "It seems like we can't win. If we live our lives through them, that's not good enough. If we tell them what we think, that's not good enough, either."

The three sat silent for a moment.

"It's different with you and Bert," Soledad said. "You talk to each other. It's not like it was with Fidel and me. I'd talk, but he never listened because he didn't think I had anything worth saying."

Simona chimed in, "And I made mine listen even if he didn't want. Maybe he had his puta because she didn't talk much."

"But Bert listens to you. The truth is, he knows you're smarter than he is," Soledad said. "The important thing is that he respects you. Yes, I know, we're all googly-eyed and in love at first, but you and Bert have grown up together and been friends and in love so long, and he still respects you."

Pedo walked in just then and darted for a piece of coffee-drenched bread under Simona's chair.

"Ay, Dios mío. Pedo! Vete. Get out of here," Soledad bolted for her broom. But Pedo slinked out of the kitchen before she could reach it.

"That dog," she said.

"What do you expect, he's a man and he wants what he wants when he wants it," Simona chuckled. The three laughed.

"So, you're saying we shouldn't wait on our husbands hand and foot?" Angie asked when the laughter subsided.

"I don't know, mija. I enjoyed doing that, and if there's ever another man in my life"—she wasn't about to tell them about Sergeant Benny—"then I think I'd still enjoy it. It's when they make you feel you're more a servant than a— ¿cómo se dice?—a partner or a friend. And I think that's true even in the making of love," Soledad added, blushing.

Simona took the napkin holder and started fanning herself. The three laughed again.

"What do you mean?" Angie asked.

Soledad, blushing more, continued. "Well, I had my chores. I cleaned house. When the boys were babies, I changed their diapers. I washed dishes. I shopped. I made love with Fidel. It was just another job. I did it *for* him and he did it *to* me. But we didn't do it together. I did that chore because that's what my mother said you did for the man you love. But it was never *for* me, because my mother said only putas enjoyed the making of love. I now think she was wrong."

"I *know* she was," Angie said suddenly, blushing when the other women laughed.

"At first," Simona said, "I thought like you did because that's what my mother said, too. But making love can also be a tool to keep your man close. My man was like putty in my hands when I paid that kind of attention to him, when it was my idea. They like that because it makes them feel wanted. But I didn't start thinking that way until after he had his puta. And when I saw how good I made him feel, that made me feel good too.

"Can I tell you a secret?" Simona continued in hushed tones. "Esos, cómo se dice, orgasmos feel good." It was Simona's turn to blush.

Soledad was not going to offer her own fairly recent experiences on the topic, but she thought Simona very wise.

The three heard Pedo whining at the front door.

"Gabby's home," Soledad said.

Gabby threw his books on the couch and came into the kitchen, Pedo bounding after him.

"Hi, Tía. Hi, Angie. What are you three laughing at? I could hear you all the way down the block."

"Nothing, mijo, we were just have a little cafecito," Soledad said, hugging Gabby.

After the three women fussed over the little man—forgetting for the moment that today they belonged to the men-are-shits club—he foraged for food, settling on a soda and a box of Trix . He left to sit in front of the television.

"Do your homework," Soledad shouted after him.

"I will, Mom," he answered.

The three sat, deep in thought about how they got along with the men in their lives.

"You know Henry and that Dolores have been seeing each other. He thinks I don't know," Simona said.

"I don't think we should be so hard on her," Soledad offered, surprising Simona.

"But she stole your man. She's a whore."

"No, she didn't steal him. He gave himself to her and took himself away from us. I don't think she's too different from the rest of us. She thought she found someone she could love and who loved her. Maybe she was a little babosa for thinking she could trust a married man who cheats, but I don't blame her too much anymore. Maybe she would be good for Henry."

Simona rolled her eyes and shot Soledad a raspberry.

"Yes, and our family parties will be very interesting," she said. "Don't ask me to forgive her. I never will."

May 1969

When the divorce decree arrived, Soledad took it to the bathroom, closed the door, sat on the toilet, and cried.

"It's what I wanted," she tried to convince herself, sobbing.

Gabby banged on the door.

"Mom, what's the matter? Are you OK?" Gabby had come running when he heard the deep sobs.

"It's nothing, mijo. I'm fine. I'll be out in a little bit."

In an apartment just over the 16th-Street bridge, Fidel was reading his copy.

He wondered why he wasn't happy.

Soledad guessed it was the finality of it all. She didn't understand all the words, but she understood what the paper represented. Her attorney had given her notice that the document would be arriving and what it meant.

The child support payments had begun long before. Fidel was also still making the house payments, though he did get to keep the car. She wondered how he paid his rent, sometimes almost feeling sympathy for Fidel.

She got the job as a seamstress at Harris, so money wasn't a problem. Benny's letters cheered her when they came, though she realized she was getting only half-truths about the war and the toll it was taking on him and Bert. Bert's letters to her were similarly guarded, but Angie shared some of the letters Bert had written her. Between the varying reports, Soledad concluded that war really was hell.

She knew she loved Benny, so why was she crying?

"Mamá, please come out. I don't like it when you cry. Please. Dad's coming to pick me up soon."

Ay, Dios, she thought. That's all I need.

Fidel and she had been civil enough to each other but

hadn't had much by way of conversation since the breakup. Fidel would know why she was crying. Maybe that would give rise to false hopes.

Gabby provided her with a running report on his apartment, whether there were any signs of women around—there weren't—and how Fidel was doing. He had quit drinking. That surprised Soledad. He had slimmed down and let his sideburns grow. He was working out at the Y.

She tried to ask the questions surreptitiously, but Gabby understood that, though his parents were apart, they still cared about one another.

And when Fidel got Gabby alone, he also slipped in roundabout questions designed to determine how Soledad was and whether she was seeing any men.

To their credit, neither one of them cut down the other in front of Gabby.

"I'll be out in a minute, mijo." She washed her face and looked in the mirror. She looked fine, she thought.

Fidel arrived about fifteen minutes later.

"Hi, Soledad," he said. "¿Cómo estás?"

"Fine. I'm fine, and you?"

Usually the talk was superficial, anything to avoid unpleasantness. This time was different, though.

"Gabby, can I talk to your mom for a few minutes?"

Stunned but hopeful, Gabby said, "Sure," and went outside to wait.

Soledad was equally stunned, but curious.

They sat on the couch.

An awkward silence followed. Fidel was having difficulty getting started.

"Did you get your papers?" Soledad asked finally, breaking the silence.

Fidel nodded.

"But that's not what I wanted to talk about."

Silence again.

"Is it about the money? I know it's a lot, and since I'm working now, it would be OK if you wanted to cut it down un poco."

"No, the money's fine. I want you and Gabby to have everything you need," he said simply.

Soledad could tell he meant it.

Fidel started to say something else, but stopped, then he said it softly, so softly that Soledad didn't catch it.

"I didn't hear what you said."

"I said, I'm sorry."

At first Soledad didn't think she heard him right. "You're sorry? ¿Por qué? What? Why?"

"I'm sorry for what I did to you. Gabby. Bert. The family."

Soledad blurted, "Fidel, we can't get back together." She regretted it instantly, seeing the hurt in Fidel's eyes.

"No," he said softly. "I know. That's not why I'm saying I'm sorry."

He paused again, looking at his shoes.

"Soledad, I've had a lot of time to think about what's important in life. You think you know. You get married. You get a good job. You raise kids, and you know in the back of your head all that stuff is important. But I forgot. I was so worried about being a man that I forgot what being a man— a good person—was about.

"I was so worried about the wrong things that I forgot how easy it is to hurt the people you love. I'm so sorry," he said, putting his face into his hands.

Soledad didn't know what to do or say. She was not accustomed to this kind of emotion—any emotion—from Fidel.

Fidel lifted his face and continued, his eyes moist, "That's what I want to tell you. All those years we were married I forgot what was important. I forgot about how I thought of you when we first got married.

"I remember loving you so much. Going to pick you up

for a date at your tía's house and wanting to tell you things about how I felt, but not being able to because, well, I never learned how to talk about those things. I couldn't share how much you meant to me then, and I forgot how much you meant to me later.

"I mean, I couldn't have been much back then. I don't want to embarrass you, but you thought I was all experienced. I wasn't. It was just a front."

"You didn't have to tell me that you loved me," Soledad said. "I knew it, but it would have been nice to hear. Sabes, I didn't tell you either."

"Yes, you did. You told me every time you made my favorite dinner. Every time you had a baby and when you lost those babies. I knew you didn't really want more babies after the first miscarriage, and you were going through the pain because I wanted another son."

"But," Soledad said, "I didn't know how to show you in the ways you thought were important. I'm sorry too."

Fidel pondered that. "You mean the other woman? I've thought a lot about why I did that. Yeah, it was nice having someone make goo-goo eyes at me."

Soledad laughed, easing the tension.

"But the more I think on it, that was my weakness, not yours. You never said no. And I guess I was flattered that someone would think about me that way, but it was my weakness that made me have to have that. I think they call it ego. I guess I never grew up. I worry if I ever will. That's all. I'm sorry I hurt you."

More silence. Gabby was outside, his ear to the door. He couldn't hear a damn thing.

"I need to tell you something too, Fidel. There's been somebody else."

Fidel just nodded, but she could tell he was hurt. She wondered if that was what she intended.

"It was after I caught you and Dolores but before you left. I'm sorry, too."

Fidel nodded again. "I guess, I'm not one who can say anything about that. I'm not the one who can judge. Are you still seeing him?"

"It's Sergeant Benny." She saw his shock. "It just happened. I needed a friend and it became more than we expected."

"Bert's letters are all about the sergeant," Fidel said, understanding some things now. "He's taking care of my boy."

Soledad nodded. "And you? I heard you and Dolores aren't together. Is there someone?"

"No, not really," Fidel told her. "There have been some women, but nothing ever grows from it."

Soledad could see his loneliness and knew now why he came without fail for Gabby every weekend and often asked for extra time during the week. She always obliged because she knew how much Gabby loved his father. In truth, she was grateful for the time alone and glad that Fidel was not the kind of cabrón the other divorced women at work were always ragging on. There seemed to be a lot of divorced women at work.

She decided if it wasn't for his camote, Fidel would be a very good man.

"That's all I wanted to tell you. I'd better go or Gabby and me will be late. I'm taking him to an Angels game. They were giving away tickets at work. We'll be home a little late."

He got up to go.

"Fidel," Soledad said. He stopped. "Gracias."

July 1969

They traveled silently through the greenery. Bert walked the point, watching for trip wires and bamboo stakes while trying to work his peripheral vision for all it was worth.

It was hard to believe he was now an old hand.

Bert stopped, holding up his hand to signal for Sergeant Benny and the rest of the squad to stop. Every time Bert worked the point, Benny's heart was in his throat.

Bert went ahead slowly, crouching and sweeping the area with his rifle.

He saw the entrance to the hole, not covered up as well as it should be.

He held up one finger, the signal for Sergeant Benny to come forward.

He pointed at the hole. Benny nodded. Bert moved to uncover the hole, but Benny shook his head.

He motioned Bert back to the squad. He got on all fours, reaching for a long stick. He got down on his belly, using the stick to uncover the hole.

The loud boom sent the squad for cover. When they looked up, they saw Benny peering into the hole and motioning them forward.

"Shit, another one?" said one GI.

Bert shook his head. Someday he'd learn. He wasn't as old a hand as he thought.

They'd been out about an hour, on their way to a village reportedly being harassed by Charlie. The Viet Cong were pressuring the young men to join. The mission was to show the flag and, in keeping with a "new" pacification program, dispense gifts and provide medical care.

The old way would have been to napalm the village. Now there was no more scorched-earth policy toward the villagers, though it was difficult to tell the friendlies from a gunship or an F-14.

Despite everything, Bert still found time to appreciate the beauty of Vietnam. He'd never seen anything greener, never anything so lush. San Bernardino was desert brown, the air smoggy gray. At night, back at camp, he'd sit behind the barracks and just stare at the stars. So many of them.

Sometimes Benny would join him and they would both just sit, looking up, thinking of home. Angie, Soledad, Fidel, and Gabby seemed so far away.

The patrol neared the village. Bert knew they'd enter tentatively, assuring themselves that these indeed were friendlies.

The ARVN—the South Vietnamese regulars—shouted what Bert guessed were encouraging words, beckoning the villagers to come out of hiding. They waved gifts and told the villagers they were there to help. Still, it took nearly a half-hour for the first villager to peer out. Once one came out and others saw he hadn't been shot, the rest came.

Sergeant Benny told the patrol to relax, though he posted sentries at both ends of the village and on an overlooking hill.

Bert plunked himself down on a grassy spot in the middle of the village. Benny sat down next to him. "That was pretty stupid back there," he said gently. "How many times do I have to tell you about those holes? Most of them are rigged." But he wasn't angry, just teaching Bert the way he was always teaching Bert.

"Yeah. I wasn't thinking."

Soon children came. They shyly sidled up to the soldiers, pointing at this and that and giggling.

"They're not so different from us," Bert said as he handed a candy bar to one little girl, who took it and ran. "If this were back home, they'd all be hanging out at Gus's, scamming for soda and candy."

A woman came carrying a baby, with the little girl who had taken the candy in tow. She said something to the little girl, who reluctantly tried to give the candy bar back to Bert. Bert shook his head, smiled at the woman, and pushed the candy bar back at the little girl. The woman said something, but Bert didn't understand.

He smiled again and pushed the candy at the little girl. The woman's face softened. She smiled and said something else to the little girl.

"Thank you," the girl said softly.

Bert smiled, "You're welcome."

She ran away. The woman was about to follow, but Bert motioned her to stop and pointed to the baby. He put down his rifle and made the universal cradling sign.

The woman—Bert figured she was about Angie's age—looked suspiciously at him. She was about five feet, two inches, just like Angie, and she carried what Bert guessed was another little girl.

Bert pulled a picture from his pocket. In it, Angie was smiling from a hospital bed, holding their little girl, María. She'd been born about a month ago.

The woman looked at the photo and smiled. She handed the baby to Bert.

Gently, Bert cradled the baby, afraid he was going to drop her.

He made faces and funny noises. The baby gurgled and laughed. He wiggled his lips and nose at the little girl and she laughed some more.

She reached up and clutched his Virgen medallion. She wasn't going to let go, it seemed. The mother saw Bert's predicament and pried the fingers loose. The baby cried until Bert started making cooing noises. The tears abruptly turned to smiles.

After the woman left, Benny looked away. He didn't have

to see Bert to know that his eyes were moist as he looked at his photo of Angie and María.

Soledad's letters to Benny had been full of the news about the baby. Benny was beginning to feel like he was part of the family, though he had to enlist some help from others to read some of Soledad's Spanish scribbling. Benny's Spanish was terrible, more Spanglish than Spanish.

"María looks just like a Rivera and so happy," she wrote in the letter Benny now read.

"She was born early in the mañana, about 3 A.M. Lucky, I didn't have to work the next day. Angie's labor took almost seven hours but she was strong. Her agua got broken the day before when she was visiting. We called the doctor and he said to come if labor started. It started about an hour later and Angie's padres took her, me, and Gabby to the hospital.

"She's so beautiful. I love my sons, but I sometimes wish I had a daughter. I guess now with Angie and María, I do. I'm so happy right now."

Benny was always touched by the simple words that conveyed so much. He was touched even more that, even as joy occurred in her family, she thought of him.

He thought back to his promise to keep Bert safe. He was working hard at it, and Bert was a natural student. Athletic and street smart, he had the makings of a top soldier, Benny thought.

Still there had been close calls, like the one this morning.

"Is that a letter from Mom?" Bert asked. Bert had long before guessed that Benny had called his mother "Sally" on the battlefield months before for a reason. As combat forged closeness, Benny confided to Bert that he was deeply in love.

Benny folded up the letter, put it back in his pocket, and nodded. "She was telling me about María."

"It's funny how we're together like this," Bert said. "I'm here with you, and back home Mom is thinking of you." There was no recrimination in the statement. "I guess joining the Army started a lot of balls rolling."

Benny nodded. "I think my life started again when you joined."

They were honest with each other this way. Bert found himself wishing he could have been as honest with his own father. Every time he thought of Fidel, he felt a little guilty for liking Sergeant Benny so much, even though Fidel had written and in a roundabout way told Bert he knew about Benny and Soledad and had given his blessing. Another letter simply apologized for what he had been and what he'd done. If the letters were any indication, Pop had changed dramatically.

Bert relied on Gabby's letters to fill in the gaps. Soledad wrote of innocuous, soothing things. Fidel's letters were awkward. Angie's letters were all about the baby and the future. But Gabby wrote about Soledad crying when the divorce papers came, about Fidel growing sideburns, and, more importantly, about his own difficulties.

Joey Villegas, a Royal Lord and a neighborhood tough, had been stabbed in a brawl on Mt. Vernon. Bert had always known Joey was destined to be stabbed, shot, or jailed. Gabby wrote eloquently, it seemed to Bert, of change. The neighborhood was getting rougher now that Gabby was in junior high. He told Bert of Chuchi's efforts to insulate him, but just being Chuchi's friend seemed to attract unwanted attention. Gabby was a gentle soul but had already been in more than one fight.

"I made out for the first time," Gabby wrote. "It was with Rosie Fierro. Louie says she's ugly, but I don't think so. He's just jealous. She kisses funny, with tongue and all that. It was fun."

Bert wished he could be there for Gabby.

It was time to go. Sergeant Benny wanted to make it back to the camp before nightfall. He didn't relish a night out in the jungle and neither did his squad. Too many damn mosquitoes, and night was also when Charlie seemed to be most active.

"Let's go. Get your gear," Benny shouted.

Soon the squad was trooping back to the jungle. As they left, the young mother waved goodbye to Bert and held up the baby for him to see. Bert's eyes watered, but he smiled back.

The young mother understood. Her husband was away too—fighting for the Viet Cong.

October 1969

Petra and Angie, best friends since childhood, were drifting apart. They didn't seem to mind. Each knew instinctively they had different roads to travel. Angie was married and home with her new baby. Petra was at the University of California, Riverside, studying premed.

Petra worried about her cousin's wife, even as she enjoyed her new life. Angie had had such plans and such potential, she thought. These plans had included marriage, but she was also going to be a nurse. Pursuit of that goal had to wait while Bert was in Vietnam and until the baby grew older.

Still, Angie and Petra enjoyed their time together. Angie had chosen tradition while Petra had chosen progress, but each still loved the other.

As Petra, Angie, Soledad, and Tía Simona cooed over the new baby, generations collided but merged in one simple truth: women had babies. In a ritual as old as mankind, women still offered solidarity, shared the joy, and gave support at such times.

Tía Simona had been born in a small shack off Mt. Vernon. She gave birth to Henry in another old shack about a mile away. Soledad was born in a rural village in Mexico, midwives and her older sisters helping her mother deliver number 6. Soledad's sons were born in an antiseptic hospital room at St. Bernardine's Hospital, where María, the newest addition to the Rivera household, also entered the world.

Petra was in awe of the whole process. She had submerged the maternal part of her womanhood in favor of academic pursuits. She had only recently lost her virginity, to a white boy. Angie was the only one who knew.

As she held María, Petra was surprised, and a little dismayed, by maternal longings. "Qué chulita," she cooed, holding the baby against her breast.

The other women looked at each other.

"Pues, mija, someday soon for you. Espero." I hope, said Simona, nodding her head.

"Not anytime soon, Tía," Petra answered as she continued snuggling the baby.

"Y ¿por qué no?" Why not, Simona asked, incredulous.

"There's time for that later. Right now I don't think my professors would understand."

"¿Profesores?" Simona said, now shaking her head. "When I was your age, I was married and with a child. Soledad, la misma. It's time to grow up. I keep telling your mother."

Petra and Angie looked at one another. Each was now accustomed to Tía Simona's rantings about familial responsibility.

"Tía, I'm very happy for you. For you, it was the right thing to do. For me, school and being a doctor is the right thing to do."

Petra put the baby down in the bassinet that Soledad had dug out of storage for just such visits from Angie and María.

"Some cafecito?" Soledad asked, trying to head off Simona.

They trooped to the kitchen and took their places at the Formica table.

Simona wasn't giving up easily. "Mija, don't you see how happy Angie is? She knows a woman's job."

Petra made a rude sound with her lips. "It's a woman's job only because men don't have the right equipment."

"And who are you to argue with how Dios made us," Simona said.

Soledad calmly poured the coffee. This was old hat to her.

"C'mon, Tía, I don't want to argue. I get this stuff from Mamá all the time anyway. It's funny, Daddy understands better than all of you, and he's a man."

"That's because he doesn't have a son and he wants you to be one to him," Simona said knowingly. She looked to Soledad for support.

Soledad sighed; she was on Petra's side. "Pues, I think Petra knows her own mind." She was going to let it go at that but thought better of it. "And you know, I like the idea of a woman doing what we all thought was a man's job."

Now Simona made a rude sound.

"Wait, listen. I've been on my own, without a man, for more than a year now, and I know one thing. Men like you to think you can't do the same things they do, but now I know different." Soledad was no longer just a seamstress. She now got to go out and measure the customers for alterations to their clothes.

"There are things I miss about not having a man around, but sabes que now at least I can read a checkbook. I pay bills. I work. All those things Fidel made me think I couldn't do. He never *tole* me I couldn't, but because he did them all the time and never taught me how, I thought I couldn't. I thought it wasn't my job."

"Pues, then what do you need a man for?" Simona asked.

"Tía! You know what men are for," Petra said, laughing.

"Ay, mija, wait till I tell your mother," Simona said, but she was laughing too.

"I think you can have both," Angie said after the chortling died down. "I mean, after Bert comes back I'm going to Valley to get my nursing degree. I know I will."

"When Bert comes back, you'll be pregnant again within a week," Petra said, still in a teasing mood.

Angie blushed and playfully slapped Petra's arm. "No, not this time. This time I'm—we're—going to be careful. We'll wait a while for the next one."

They each sipped their coffees. Angie kept a sharp ear out for crying, her signal to feed the baby.

Different generations with different expectations.

*   *   *

Across town, Dolores and Henry were talking.

Since her breakup with Fidel, Dolores had actively pursued Fidel's cousin, Henry. At first, it was to get back at Fidel. As the relationship progressed, however, Dolores began to see beyond Henry's butterball chubbiness to the bright, serious, considerate man underneath. More importantly, he offered something Dolores had never experienced before: stability.

"Henry, how come you've never let me meet your mother?" she asked. They were sitting in Dolores's kitchen after making love. At first, Henry, deeply religious, had been reluctant on that score, but he came around. Dolores enjoyed teaching him.

"Pues, you know why, mija." She loved the way he called her mija.

"You and my family got too much history. You know, you and Fidel."

"Didn't that ever bother you?" Dolores asked. "I mean, he's your cousin. Does it bother you that I was with other men before you?"

Henry thought about it. "I guess it did at first, but what's important is that you're with me now and that you want to be."

She reached over and caressed his cheek. "Es cierto." That's true, she said. "But I don't always understand why you want to be with me. I mean, I haven't been a very good person." Her eyes glistened, and she looked down at the Pepsi in her glass.

"I think you're wonderful," he said simply.

"Let's go back to bed," Dolores said hopefully.

Henry laughed and said they'd have to wait a little bit. "Chico needs his rest." That's the name they gave his camote. Dolores hadn't realized that a woman could have such honest, heartfelt conversations with a man. Henry returned to the original topic.

"I don't know. I always wanted you, but I saw Fidel had you. It goes back to when we were kids—Fidel, me, and the other cousins. I wasn't like them. They were always good at sports and at getting women. I wasn't and they let me know it. I was good at school so they called me 'white boy.' It was like that all through our lives.

"Did you know I met Soledad, Fidel's wife, first. It was at church. She was so pretty and I didn't know what to say. I just watched as Fidel moved in and swept her off her feet.

"And then you came to me. That was what was important. You wanted me. I didn't have to take any chances."

He saw Dolores wince.

"I know it sounds hard, as if I wanted you just because Fidel had you before, but that's not how it was. I loved you before you and Fidel got together. You just didn't know it. You could've been with him for ten years and I still would've wanted you, but Fidel always got there first and I couldn't compete."

Dolores took his face in her hands. "I need to tell you. I came to you to hurt Fidel. I'm sorry. Now I know you're the man I've always wanted but never gave myself to. I made so many mistakes."

Henry nodded. "I know, and it doesn't matter."

"But now," Dolores said, "I love you and don't think I could ever be with another man."

Henry smiled. "I know."

They each drank their Pepsis in silence for a while.

"You know Santa Fe is cutting back here in San Bernardino."

She nodded. She had heard such talk among the Santa Fe patrons at the restaurant.

"They want me to move. They're offering a promotion, but I have to go to Barstow."

Dolores's eyes grew frightened. "What are you saying? You're leaving?"

"Not without you, mija. Never without you."

Dolores thought on that. "What are you really saying?"

"Will you marry me?"

Dolores shrieked, scurried around the table, and hugged him. The box Henry was digging out of his pocket dropped to the floor.

She picked it up. "¿Qué es?" What is it?

"Open it."

Inside were two rings. One had large stones. The other was simpler, a gold band with pin-drop jewels imbedded.

Dolores cried. "But your mother. I know you love your mother. She'll never accept me."

"I'm not marrying my mother. She'll have to understand or never see her grandkids. Does that mean the answer is yes?"

She hugged him again as he pondered how to tell his mother. It wouldn't be easy.

Later, Soledad wondered at the shouting and shrieking coming from Henry's house.

"Mamá, it's what I want. I'm a grown man."

"Then act like one," Simona shouted. "She's a puta who destroyed your cousin's home."

"Shut up!"

Silence. Never in his life had Henry ever spoken to her so harshly.

"If I ever hear you call her that again, you won't see me or your grandkids. Ever."

Grandkids? "Is there something you're not telling me? Has she trapped you by getting pregnant? Qué baboso eres."

"No, Mamá. She's not pregnant. But I wouldn't mind if she was. Listen, you have some choices to make. It won't be a big wedding—I won't pretend Fidel never happened and invite the rest of the family—but I do want you there. You make up your own mind. If you're there, you're there. If you're not, don't ever expect to see me again."

Simona was flabbergasted. Henry left her standing like that as he went to his room to pack. He would live his last week of bachelorhood with the woman he loved.

A week later, Simona was at the wedding. The bigger surprise: so was Soledad. They each walked up to the bride and gave her a long, lasting embrace.

"Bienvenido a la familia," was all Soledad said. Welcome to the family.

October 17, 1969:
Gabby's Night Out

They'd planned for weeks. Gabby and Louie, knowing
better than their mothers that they were no longer children,
were going to pull an all-nighter. It was a Friday night.
Soledad went to bed early, about nine, and Gabby would
sneak out. Simple.

They would, with Chuchi and his car, go to Kaiser Dome
for a dance. The famous Jades were playing.

Gabby, already sprouting peach fuzz on his upper lip, was
confident he could fool curfew-conscious cops.

In the car, Louie was getting nervous. "If we get caught,
Gabby, we're in deep shit. And how do you know Rosie is
going to be there?"

"C'mon, Louie, nothing's going to happen."

Chuchi didn't have a license but had long ago got a car of
sorts—a blue '53 Buick that ran roughly but got him where
he wanted to go. Wanting to tame down his life a bit, he left
the Lords in favor of a fledgling car club, The Regals. The
Regals had fourteen members, but only three had cars. The
Lords hadn't wanted Chuchi to leave but by now were much
too aware of his fighting skills to argue.

The dance was sponsored by the Chancellors, who knew
that such an event also tended to attract unsavory elements—
enough to spoil any good time for the majority who were
there only to dance, socialize, and score.

Rosie Fierro was sitting along the wall, waiting to be asked
to dance. She and Gabby eyed one another. Gabby, muster-
ing his courage, told himself he would wait for a slow one.

The next one was slow.

"Would you like to dance, Rosie?" he asked tentatively.

Rosie, stunning it seemed to Gabby in a white blouse with a low neckline and pleated skirt, smiled an endearing and toothy smile and nodded.

He took her hand and led her to the dance floor.

Cheek to cheek, pelvis to pelvis, they danced that dance and the next three.

Gabby figured he'd make his move. "Would you like to go outside?" he asked nonchalantly.

"OK."

Rosie, only thirteen but already wise to the ways of boys, thanks to older sisters, knew he wanted to make out. So did she. She liked Gabby a lot. The notes passed in school, unbeknownst to Gabby, were all about him. Odds were three to one that she would snag him before semester's end. What Rosie didn't know was that Chuchi's car was unlocked. Gabby had access to a back seat.

They walked and talked for a while until they reached Chuchi's car.

"You want to sit awhile? This is Chuchi's car."

Rosie raised an eyebrow but agreed. At least it was private.

Gabby had been asking questions of Chuchi earlier. "Chuchi, is there, like, a spot on a girl where if you touch it, it drives her crazy?"

Chuchi explained about a little button above the vagina. Gabby pretended he understood but wasn't quite sure how he was supposed to get that far. Besides, how far above the vagina? To the belly button? Gabby didn't fully understand female anatomy despite Bert's hidden *Playboys*.

"Aw, man, that's sick," said Louie.

It didn't sound so sick to Gabby.

In the back seat of the car, Gabby and Rosie got down to business right away. She, after all, had already taught him how to French-kiss. Tonight she would move on to Hickeys 101.

Gabby was breathing hard as she nibbled his neck, but his head wasn't so far gone that he didn't know where he wanted his hand to go.

His hand, which had been resting on her hip, slipped slowly upward to her breast.

She gasped, "Gabby, no."

His hand retreated as they continued kissing.

Soon, however, his hand slid up again. This was Chuchi's advice. First get her used to the idea of hand-to-breast contact, then move lower.

Rosie protested more weakly this time, since he now nibbled on her neck as she had just taught him. She didn't move his hand, anyway.

She was breathing harder, and Gabby wasn't far behind.

The windows were fogging from all the CO_2 expended.

He moved his hand lower, to her hip again. To his surprise, she took his hand and brought it back to her breast. He cupped the small breast, squeezed, and felt for the nipple, as Chuchi had advised.

Her breathing grew even more ragged.

She pushed him away. "Wait, we're going too fast."

Gabby just looked at her with wide, brown puppy eyes. She smiled and reached out again.

His hand slipped from her hip to her lower thigh. She didn't seem to notice that his hand rested just below the hem of her skirt.

Gabby's hand inched its way up. Rosie's breathing grew faster. She offered one weak protest but did nothing to stop him. His hand went under her skirt, parting her legs slightly, and found its target. She gasped as his fingers reached the wet spot on her panties.

"No, Gabby, not yet. We're not even going steady," she said as she pulled away and smoothed her skirt.

Gabby leaned back against the car door. "Don't beg,"

Chuchi had said, but Gabby was on the verge of doing just that. His camote was stretched hard against his pants.

"Oh, Rosie, I want you so much." He reached for her and she came to him. They began kissing and nibbling, but she stopped him when his hand started roaming again.

"Do you love me?" she asked.

"More than anything," Gabby answered, and it didn't seem to him that he was lying. Then, in what seemed like a solemn moment to them both, Gabby reached up to the St. Christopher medal hanging from his neck. He put it around her neck.

"Now we're going steady," he said.

Rosie's eyes grew misty and their lips met again.

The kissing continued, but petting was as far as it got. That's as far as Rosie was going to let it go. She had plans for Gabby and getting pregnant at age thirteen wasn't among them.

Still, when they emerged from the car, Gabby walked with a little swagger.

When they got back to the dance, Rosie's girlfriends eyed her knowingly. Her older sister, Lupe, cast an evil glance Gabby's way. All of them marveled at the St. Christopher medal around her neck, even as they noticed the hickeys just starting to blossom.

Louie leaned against a wall, trying very hard to look cool.

"Hey, Louie, guess what? Rosie and me are going steady."

"Where you been, man? You left me all alone."

"Aw, c'mon, Louie, you're supposed to be asking girls to dance."

"I did," he lied.

"You haven't even danced yet, I bet."

Louie started to protest, but Gabby cut him short. "Guess what else?"

He turned his back to where Rosie was showing off the St.

Christopher medal to her girlfriends. In the background, the Jades played a soulful version of "I'm Your Puppet."

"This hand has been where it had no business going."

Louie's eyes grew wide. "Did you get laid?"

But Gabby now remembered another piece of advice offered by both Bert and Chuchi: don't brag, especially if it's true, por vida, love. And that's what it felt like just then.

"Uh, never mind."

Louie was unsatisfied. "Oh, vato, you're not going to tell me, are you? Shit."

Gabby saw Chuchi walking toward them. He could tell something was wrong.

"C'mon, let's go. We got to get out of here."

"Why, what's happening?" Louie asked.

"C'mon, I'll tell you vatos on the way out."

Gabby stopped to tell Rosie that he had to leave. She pouted, but they kissed in front of people. That's when everyone knew it was serious.

He was smiling as he walked out with Chuchi and Louie.

Louie was still asking questions. "What's the matter?"

"Some Colton guys are here and they've seen me. They went out to get some more vatos," Chuchi said as they jumped into the car. "We gotta go."

As the car pulled out of the parking lot, another car pulled out behind them.

"Shit. They saw us," said Chuchi, looking into the rear-view mirror.

"Shit," echoed Gabby and Louie.

"Let's go to the police station," offered Louie.

"Fuck, are you crazy? I don't even have a driver's license. Besides, they like when we kill each other," Chuchi said as he pushed the pedal to the floor and headed downtown where there were more people.

A shot rang out. Louie and Gabby, wide-eyed, scooted to the floorboard.

"Man, what was that?" Gabby asked.

"Just the car backfiring," Chuchi explained.

The car rattled. It was being asked to do something it was ill equipped to do—go fast. The other car gained on them.

Suddenly, Chuchi's car started sputtering and coughing. "Shit."

He turned quickly. Seccombe Park loomed ahead of them. The car went dead.

"Get out! Run to the lake."

Gabby, Bert, and Fidel had spent many a summer evening at this park hauling out fishing poles to catch the little tikes in the lake just to throw them back.

Now it seemed dark and foreboding.

Behind them, car doors slammed and vatos shouted.

"Where'd they go?"

"There. Over there."

The trio knew they wouldn't reach the lake. Chuchi's plan was to silently swim to the small island in the middle of the lake and wait the Colton vatos out.

They ducked into an alley separating the concession stand from the restrooms.

Pointy shoes with taps on the heels went clicking past. From the racket, Chuchi guessed there were at least five of them. He held his finger to his lips.

"Listen, we're going to have to make it to the island. We'll wait there until they leave. The chota comes here a lot because the Lords drink beer here sometimes. They chase us out all the time. If the Colton guys see us and start chasing us, you guys keep going. I'm the one they want. I kicked that crazy Flaco's ass at the Orange Show. He said he'd get me but when I was with the Lords he was too scared to do anything. Now's his chance."

"We shouldn't leave you, Chuchi," Gabby said.

"Listen, don't take this wrong, but you guys aren't going

to be much help if it comes to chingazos. These guys are like eighteen or nineteen years old."

"We shouldn't leave you," Gabby insisted.

Louie nodded. "Yeah. We can help."

"Let's talk about it later. Let's try to get to the lake."

Silently, they made for the water. They were midway when they heard footsteps coming up behind them. The Colton vatos had split up. Three of them came straight for Chuchi.

"Run!" Chuchi yelled.

Louie grabbed Gabby's arm and dragged him toward the lake. Almost to the lake, Gabby noticed Chuchi wasn't with them.

"Wait, we can't leave him," Gabby said.

"What can we do?" Louie asked.

In the distance they could hear fighting, blows followed by grunts. Chuchi would be getting the worst of that.

Gabby looked around. By the pier were loose two-by-fours.

"Here, take this," he said, throwing one at Louie. "C'mon."

The four were still fighting. Two held Chuchi while the other rained blows on him. Chuchi was kicking and trying to get free.

Gabby and Louie flailed with the boards. Gabby's first swing caught one Colton vato on the shoulder blades. He let go of Chuchi and went down on all fours. He looked up at Gabby just in time to catch a blow across the cheek. He was out.

Louie took his Colton vato down with a swing to his knee. He went down immediately and started crawling away, shouting as he did.

Meanwhile, Chuchi focused his attention on Flaco.

Something flashed and Gabby heard Chuchi grunt as he grabbed his side and went down. Flaco landed on top of Chuchi, about to cut him again, but Gabby swung as hard as he could with the two-by-four and cracked Flaco's wrist. Screaming like a girl, he rolled off. As he lay flat on his back,

Gabby hit him again in the midsection. He just curled up in fetal position and moaned.

"C'mon, Chuchi. We got to get out of here. There are two more. They'll be on their way."

Chuchi got up slowly, clutching a red mass on his side.

"Shit," Louie said. "Is it bad?"

"Bad enough."

They each grabbed Chuchi and made for the lake.

"We got to do this quiet," Gabby said.

"You vatos go. I don't know if I can swim like this," Chuchi said.

"We'll help," Louie said. Both Louie and Gabby had taken advanced Red Cross swimming lessons, at their fathers' insistence.

They slid into the water. Gabby and Louie each swam slowly at Chuchi's side.

"I'm not going to make it," Chuchi said.

"Dammit. Don't give up," Gabby said between gulps of water.

Chuchi went under. Louie and Gabby went down for him, grabbed an arm, and sidestroked as they pulled Chuchi along.

Signs around the small lake sternly prohibited swimming, and Gabby had often wondered what it would be like to swim to the island where the duck and geese hung out when they weren't scarfing down bread and other treats from the park's visitors. The island seemed so close from the other side. Now it seemed like swimming the English Channel.

Finally, they reached the island. Gabby and Louie pulled Chuchi ashore. Around them, ducks and geese noisily awoke and escaped to the water. A couple of geese gave challenge but loudly gave up after Louie slung rocks at them.

"Shit, I hope those Colton guys didn't hear anything," Louie said as the last goose slid into the water, still honking.

Off in the distance, however, the Colton vatos were in full retreat. A car started up and roared away.

A few minutes later, they saw blue and red flashing lights where Chuchi had stopped his car.

Chuchi lay on his back, still holding his side.

"Let me see," Gabby said, pulling Chuchi's hand away. "Shit, you're bleeding bad. It's deep."

"Here," Louie said, taking off his T-shirt and putting it on the wound. "You remember, Gabby. You got to apply pressure."

"We got to get him to a hospital or he's going to bleed to death. Going through this dirty water probably didn't help."

"No, I can't go to the hospital. They'll ask what happened. We'll all go to juvie," Chuchi protested.

"Not if we get our stories straight now," Gabby said. "Look, here's what happened. Listen, Louie! Our car broke down at the park. Some guys jumped us as we walked to the telephone at the soda stand to call my mom. We beat them off but had to swim to the island to get away. That way, we're the victims. We didn't get a good look at them. There were five of them. They drove off in a white '56 Chevy. OK? We were too busy to get a license number. They were all short Mexicans with white T-shirts on. We don't give good descriptions."

It made sense, Chuchi thought. "But the car. They'll know I don't have a license."

"C'mon, Chuchi, you're not thinking right. You got to get to a hospital. Getting a ticket is better than losing your life."

Chuchi nodded.

"You stay with him. I'll go for the cops. They'll get us off the island."

Gabby slid back into the water, swimming as hard as he could, hoping that the cops wouldn't leave before he got there.

He was winded once he got to the other side. He ran to where a single cop was still talking into the radio. He'd find out the car was registered in the name of Chuchi's mom, though she didn't know it. She had signed the papers in a drunken stupor. It bothered him that the doors were wide open.

"Officer, Officer! Help us. My friend has been stabbed," Gabby said, in his best little-kid-in-peril voice.

The officer looked up, startled. "What, the . . . Settle down, tell me about it."

Gabby rattled off the story, and the officer immediately called it in. Assault with a deadly weapon, youth down. Send ambulance. Five suspects in a white '56 Chevy.

The Colton guys had actually driven off in a red '65 Ford Fairlane.

The ambulance drivers unhooked some boats at the concession stand and headed for the island, and Gabby went with them.

Chuchi was unconscious when they arrived. Louie was still holding his T-shirt to the wound.

The paramedics worked on Chuchi until they stopped the bleeding. Carefully, they loaded him onto the boat. On shore, the cops waited with the stretcher. Ten minutes later, Chuchi was in the emergency room at county hospital.

There, more cops peppered Louie and Gabby with questions. Neither of them broke.

Later, parents came. Fidel even came with Soledad. They held hands. Louie's parents came too and immediately started shouting at Louie. Chuchi's mom wouldn't be found until the next morning. She was sleeping another one off at a stranger's house.

The parents were worried at first. Later, they would demand answers. Louie, Chuchi, and Gabby never veered from their stories.

Gabby was grounded for a month—three weeks for sneaking out, one week for the hickeys. Louie got two months.

Six weeks after he got there, Chuchi emerged from the hospital, part of his stomach missing but little else to show for the incident but a deep, mean scar. That, and a friendship with Gabby and Louie that would last the rest of their lives.

The only ones who would ever know the truth about that night were Louie, Chuchi, Gabby, and, much later—after she and Gabby were married—Rosie.

July 1970:
The Last Firefight

Corporal Bert Rivera knew this was going to be a bad one.

It smelled too much like that very first firefight: some new kids just off the stateside plane joining them. This time, Bert thought, I'm not going to let anything happen to them. He remembered Gil Real and Book Johnson too well.

He had been a corporal for about two months now. Corporal Larry Philbin went out on patrol but didn't come back. He was MIA. Bert was the new corporal. That was likely Sergeant Benny's doing.

It meant more money for Angie and the baby, so Bert didn't balk, though he didn't relish the added responsibility. He had to worry about other people going home alive besides himself.

Going home.

In three more weeks, Bert would be going home. Soon after that, he and the Army would be through. He had no intention of re-upping—reenlisting.

Sergeant Benny told him that the squad was going in on a big push westward. Bert knew, as did everyone except the folks back home, that west meant Cambodia, where North Vietnamese regulars and Charlie operated with impunity.

Everyone hoped that the secret saturation bombing from the B-52s would mean little or no resistance. Benny and Bert knew better. It was going to be nasty, the equivalent of taking on the Colton vatos on their home turf.

The wump-wumping of the Huey nearly drowned out Benny's voice as he told the troops to check their rifles and their magazines. He told Cinestro, the radio man, to stick close.

"Listen up, no one takes chances. You do as I do and do as I say. You got that?"

Everyone nodded.

Along with the wump-wump of the chopper, they now heard booms.

Bert looked out the door and saw mortars exploding below.

Benny sat down next to Bert. "And you, short-timer, you just watch your ass if you want to get home alive."

"Ain't nothing coming between me and going home," Bert answered. He meant it.

Benny nodded.

Bullets starting pinging off the chopper.

"Shit, they got us. They better not have any surface-to-air down there." Second Lieutenant Golding, not long from ROTC in Iowa, was a worrier. He was green but a good officer, Bert thought. Naturally cautious, he so far had not volunteered his men for anything or landed them in too much trouble out in the boonies.

The chopper started its descent and stomachs churned and turned. A machine-gunner in the doorway started spraying the clearing and the jungle beyond with rapid fire.

The last months had been a roller coaster for Bert. Too many firefights, too many wistful nights wishing he was home, and too many newspapers read. He knew he was fighting a war that everyone just wanted to be over. A war that everyone, from the president on down, acknowledged was futile and unwinnable even if they weren't using those exact words. The generals still said they were winning, claiming inflated body counts as proof. Bert knew better.

Benny said nothing had changed from his last tour.

The Navy was looking better to Bert, and he was giving Uncle Henry some credit for smarts.

"OK, you guys, let's go," Golding said, jumping and running low to the ground. His squad wasn't far behind.

From the jungle, a shoulder-fired missile arched, sought out, and found a Huey to their right.

"Shit," Bert said as he ran behind Benny. "This ain't good." So much for surprise invasions, he thought.

Other choppers landed around them. God, there must be hundreds of guys here. From the jungle, the mortars started raining in. Just like that first time.

Destroy the enemy's supply lines. That was the rationale behind this latest operation. Give the South Vietnamese regime a few more years of life.

The lieutenant was motioning them forward. There was a flash, an explosion, and the lieutenant wasn't there anymore.

"C'mon, you guys, let's get the hell out of here!" Benny yelled as he took the squad toward the jungle.

"Hit the ground!" he shouted as another mortar slammed the ground to their right.

Amid the fire, Bert heard some crying. That would be the new guys.

He crawled over to were a soldier hugged the ground. Bert shook him by the shoulder. "OK, it's tough. OK? But we're going to get creamed if we stay out in the open. Get ready to move."

The soldier, wild-eyed with fear, simply nodded.

"You move when I tell you to move. You got that?" Bert said more roughly this time. "You just watch me. You do as I do."

This time the soldier's eyes seemed to focus. He nodded again, and Bert was certain he would follow.

Benny waved to him, his signal to move forward with his half of the squad. Withering machine-gun fire from the jungle mowed down three before they hit the ground again.

"Medic! Medic!" Benny shouted. "Get these guys out of here."

The medics split up, shook their heads at two of the bodies, and converged on the third.

"This one!" They dragged him to where the choppers first landed. Some choppers circled overhead. They were both air support and ambulance.

Benny was talking into the radio. Cinestro, an old hand, stuck close.

Bert crawled to him. "What's up?"

"We're going to pull back. Those dumb shits said light resistance. We got a whole North Vietnamese brigade here, they're saying now. We got to pull back and dig in on that hill, they say. They're going to try again with the napalm."

"Shit, Benny, how far away is the air support? If we dig in, they'll chew us up. A brigade? Shit. Shit!"

"Yeah, I know. OK, you get what's left and let's move. Let's go!" On either side of the squad, others had gotten the same message and were pulling back. What seemed like hundreds had been whittled down considerably.

From the jungle, bodies started emerging, firing their rifles, hitting the ground, then repeating.

"Here they come," Benny shouted. At least the mortars stopped. The North Vietnamese knew that to avoid the napalm they had to mix it up with the U.S. troops.

"You, you, and you. Stay with me," Benny said, motioning Bert toward him. "You get these guys to that hill. We got to buy you some time."

"I'll stay," Bert said.

"Fuck that. Get out of here," Benny answered. "We'll pull back slowly. Hey you, where you going with that M-60?"

Bert started gathering the remnants of the squad. "Let's go. Pull back. Run!"

He saw Benny and the others fire at the moving bodies. He saw other squads on either side of them split up and do the same.

The hill, actually just higher ground, loomed ahead of them. Back in the distance, Bert could barely make out

Benny's position. He saw some bodies move toward them. That would be Benny and the others.

Bert gave orders to start digging. "Dig, you assholes. You're going to need cover if Charlie makes it this far. Another missile arched from the jungle and found another chopper.

"Shit, we're getting creamed," a soldier said as he dug.

Bert started digging. Looking back he could see Benny and two others not even pretending to maneuver. They were just plain running now.

"Man oh man. This is bad," the digging soldier was saying.

"Would you shut the fuck up, Johnson. You're going to scare the new kids."

"Shit, Corporal, we're already scared," a new kid said. Another one next to him laughed, but kept on digging.

Two squad members who had been with Benny joined the group, winded.

"Where's Benny?" Bert shouted. "Where the fuck did you leave the sergeant?"

"I saw him go down, Bert. I don't think he made it." That was Cinestro.

"OK, Cinestro. Get the rest of these guys to dig in. I'm going back for him."

Overhead, the Hueys had checked the North Vietnamese advance momentarily. The enemy troops concentrated their fire on the choppers, ignoring the mauled ground troops for the time being.

Bert scampered from body to body as he made his way back, sometimes coming on an American, other times a North Vietnamese. He found Benny about halfway to where they first landed. He could hear the voices of the live North Vietnamese.

"It's my leg," Benny said, grimacing. "Shit, I'm the one who's supposed to be taking care of you."

"Shut up, Benny. You're going to piggyback."

He hauled Benny onto his feet, or actually, his foot. Bert saw the other boot was just a bloody pulp. "Climb on."

Bert got about twenty-five yards when he felt his legs give out from under him. They fell.

"Shit, too many frijoles, Benny."

"Get the fuck out of here. I'll crawl back."

"No way. Let's go, vato."

But as they looked toward the jungle, they saw the bodies moving closer, still firing.

"Hit the ground! Man, Benny. Where's your rifle?"

"Back there somewhere. I guess I'll have to owe Uncle Sam."

Benny pulled out his .45. Bert fired his M-16 and saw two go down. Dirt and grass kicked up around them.

"Don't bother with that pistol. It don't got the range."

"You shouldn't have come, Bert. I promised Sally."

Bert could tell Benny was in pain and losing blood. "Like I said, Benny, ain't nothing getting in the way of going home to Angie. We'll get there."

"I don't think so, mijo," Benny said. "Look at my leg. That's an artery that just popped."

Indeed, the blood was gushing now.

Bert got on his knees. "I'll get a tourniquet on it."

A powerful blow suddenly slammed Bert to the ground.

He tried to get up but felt a deep burning pain in his right shoulder. He used the other arm to steady himself. His right arm hung uselessly at his side. He felt warm liquid pour down under his shirt.

"How many times I got to tell you, boy. Stay down," Benny said, worry replacing the pain in his eyes.

Bert crawled to him. His rifle was where he had left it.

Benny took the rifle, turned on his belly, and fired. Two others, now closer, went down. Overhead, the choppers were the only things checking the North Vietnamese advance.

As Benny fired, Bert tried to tie a tourniquet one-handed.

Using his teeth and his one good hand, he managed it. Benny grunted when Bert tightened it.

"Medic!" Bert shouted when he was through.

"It's no use, mijo. They can't hear you. You better go back. Tourniquet or no tourniquet, I'm going to bleed to death and so are you if you don't go back."

"Shut up. I'm not going anywhere without you. C'mon, I'm going to drag you, but you got to help."

"You know, mijo, I never had a son. You're the closest I've come."

"Man, don't get sloppy on me."

Bert sat on his butt, grabbed Benny by the collar with his one good arm and pulled backward. Benny was too weak to fight but hollered from the pain.

Inch by inch, foot by foot, Bert booty-scooted Benny toward the squad's position. Benny clung to the rifle, firing a shot toward the North Vietnamese every time he got a target.

As they neared the squad's position, Bert shouted out. "We're coming in! Cinestro, you hear me?"

"I hear you, we'll come get you." Cinestro jumped from his hole but was slammed back. He didn't get back up.

Bert saw the medics running toward them.

"Let's go," one said, grabbing Benny first. "We'll come back for you."

In a fireman's carry, they hauled Benny to the dug-in positions.

Bert tried to follow, but Benny was right. He had lost too much blood.

He saw his rifle on the ground. He grabbed it and tried to fire off some shots, but the rifle just clicked. He got a fresh magazine and jammed it in with some difficulty.

He saw the jet then, swooping down on the jungle, setting it ablaze.

The two medics returned. "Your turn, let's go."

Bert was still clinging to his rifle when they loaded him, semiconscious and gritting his teeth against the pain onto the helicopter. Besides the crew, he was the only live one on the chopper.

Inside the body bag next to him was Sergeant Benny.

*   *   *

Three days later, the Army staff-car pulled up to the Rivera house on 14th Street. Soledad saw the car and her heart sank. Gabby ran to the window and turned back to Soledad, tears in his eyes. "Maybe it's OK, Mamá. He's OK."

But he didn't believe it himself.

Next door, Tía Simona also had tears in her eyes. She knew what such a visit meant.

The officer knocked on the door. Gabby answered.

"Hi, son. Is your mother or father home?"

Gabby motioned him inside. Soledad was already seated on the sofa. "Siéntese." Sit down, she said, not noticing or caring that the officer was not Mexican.

He understood and sat. "Mrs. Rivera?"

Soledad nodded.

"It's my sad duty to inform you, ma'am, that your son Umberto has been wounded."

"¿Está muerto?" Soledad asked.

The officer looked at Gabby.

"Is he alive?" Gabby offered.

"Yes, he'll be fine."

Her sobs burst out all of a sudden. Gabby walked over and hugged her. "I told you he'd be OK, Mamá. I told you."

"¿Qué pasó?" she asked the officer. Gabby translated, "What happened?"

"Corporal Rivera was helping lead his squad against hostile forces in Vietnam," the officer said. He had done this too many times before. He didn't know that the firefight was actually in Cambodia, but such distinctions would mean little to Soledad. "Another member of his squad was wounded and Corporal Rivera returned to render assistance."

He saw the puzzlement in Soledad's eyes. "He went back to help," Gabby said.

"While in pursuit of those duties and in attempting to save the life of the other squad member, Corporal Rivera was shot . . ." Soledad gasped and sobbed again. Gabby stuck close, his throat catching too.

"As I said, Corporal Rivera was shot. He suffered a serious wound to his right shoulder. His collarbone was shattered. He is in a hospital in Saigon now, recovering. Some more bad news, Mrs. Rivera. We're not certain if the corporal will regain full use of his right arm, but it's a little early to tell. We've already told his wife, the other Mrs. Rivera."

"¿Quién era el otro soldado?"

"Who was the soldier Bert was saving?" Gabby asked.

"I don't have his name, but it was his sergeant. He didn't make it," the officer said.

Soledad clutched her face in her hands and let loose deep, mournful sobs.

The officer was puzzled. "Ma'am? Did I say something wrong?"

"The sergeant was a friend," Gabby said simply, hugging his mom closer, understanding now about those hidden letters.

Gabby thanked the puzzled officer and showed him to the door.

The news traveled fast on the Rivera grapevine. First Angie, Simona, and Petra came, then other members of the family, then neighbors. Soon the house was full. They brought food and expressed their hopes that Bert would recover soon. They wondered why Soledad was so shattered, but didn't press.

Gabby could see the tíos were proud of Bert. Even Uncle Henry and his new bride, Dolores, came for a short time.

Later, after everyone left, Fidel came.

As Soledad sat at the kitchen table with her coffee in front of her, Fidel didn't say a word. He sat across from her and took her hand. He looked into her eyes and she could see he had been crying, too.

"I'm so sorry. I'm so sorry," was all he said.

They sat that way, hands clasped, for the rest of the evening.

January 1971:
Wounds Do Heal

Bert had six months in various hospitals to think about things.

He found out about Sergeant Benny while in the hospital in Saigon. He awoke in deep pain but still thought to ask about Benny. The doctors and nurses knew nothing.

It wasn't until the company commander visited that Bert found out Benny had died on the battlefield. It had been for nothing. "I've never had a son," was all he could remember of Benny's last words.

The company commander told Bert he was recommending him for a Silver Star and Benny for the Congressional Medal of Honor. Bert knew Benny would say such medals were bullshit, but that he would be secretly pleased.

Soldier to soldier, the major confided that the operation in which Benny died and Bert was wounded had been a cluster-fuck from the beginning. They had put four companies in the field against a corps of heavily equipped North Vietnamese regulars. Faulty intelligence. The misfortunes of war.

Too many good men dead. Too many men wounded.

But they were going back in, he said. "You don't need to worry about that."

Bert nodded numbly, thinking about the waste.

On the flight home from yet another hospital in Hawaii, Bert reread the letter from Soledad.

"Querido hijo:

"We are very happy you are coming home. Everyone is so proud of you, but no one more than me.

"They told me you were shot trying to save Benny's life. I know you will feel bad, thinking that maybe it is your fault.

Don't think that way. Benny was a soldier and he knew what that meant. No lo entiendo, but he was happy being a soldier.

"Maybe you don't know, but he made a promise to me to keep you safe. He did. I will love you forever for trying to save his life. I know he would be proud of you. Me and your papá are very proud of you. Come home to us pronto.

"Con mucho cariño,

"Tu Mamá."

Bert didn't know if he would be able to face his mother. It was all so complicated. He was feeling guilty for not saving the life of the man, not his father, whom his mother loved.

The doctors rebuilt his collarbone and his shoulder. There was nerve damage, and he likely wouldn't have full use of his right arm, but with a lot of physical therapy he would regain, say, about 75 percent. He wouldn't be pitching for the majors, they joked.

He just wanted his arms for hugging his wife and carrying his baby, and that's all he would be doing for a while.

His family was waiting for him at Norton Air Force Base. They peered behind the glass. They weren't allowed on the tarmac, but Bert could see their glistening eyes as he stepped off the plane.

Angie rushed toward him as he walked through the glass doors, María in her arms. The baby, with soulful brown eyes, smiled at the stranger and blew bubbles. He dropped his duffel bag and hugged Angie with his one good arm. They both cried.

María cooed and gurgled.

"Let me hold her," Bert said. He unslung his right arm and cradled her in his left. "The arm is plenty good for this," he murmured.

That was the signal. The rest of the family mobbed him. Gabby held off, bashful at first, until he couldn't wait longer and threw himself at Bert. Bert noticed that the top of the mocoso's head now came to his nose.

"Hey, it looks like at least one Rivera is going to be tall," he said.

Soledad and Fidel hung back together. They held hands and watched.

"We done good," Fidel said, slipping his arm around Soledad.

Bert caught his mother's eye.

Soledad nodded her head. Yes, we're back together. We're a family again.

Bert smiled. Fidel blushed. Bert had never seen his father blush before.

He handed the baby to Angie and walked over to Soledad and Fidel. "This is a good homecoming gift."

On 14th Street, the backyard was festooned with ribbon and a "Welcome home Bert" banner. The piñata was in its accustomed place, as was the silver keg.

It was a real pachanga.

The tíos were anxious to hear all about it but appreciated the fact that Bert wasn't ready to talk yet.

He never would be.

As the beer flowed, Tía Simona surveyed the scene and knew everything was going to be all right after all.

She knew. People change. Family endures.

Epilogue

Years later, the Rivera family traveled to Sacramento.

Fidel walked with a cane now, arthritis paying a visit since his retirement from Santa Fe. Soledad walked alongside him, a wreath of flowers on her arm. Bert, Angie, their two teenage girls—María and Sally—and the "baby" who wasn't quite a baby anymore, Benjamin, followed behind with Gabby, Rosie, and their children, David and Simona.

Petra—now Dr. Petra Rivera-Cauley—had joined them on this pilgrimage in years past, but her thriving pediatrics practice and her own growing brood—three headstrong and self-sufficient girls—prevented it this year.

Tía Simona had died the year before but not before seeing the birth of her fourth perfect grandchild, born of her perfect daughter-in-law, Dolores.

Fourteenth Street seemed a bit seedier now. Families moved on, but not Soledad and Fidel. There were too many memories.

Down the street, Chuchi had the best-manicured lawn on the block. Now that Tía Simona was gone, he had taken over as the neighborhood conscience. Using a storefront on Mt. Vernon and his own considerable experience, he worked with neighborhood youth to show them an alternative to gangs. He was successful because he bore the scars and wasn't above busting heads to get things accomplished.

Louie's glass company and Bert's string of auto body shops sponsored many of the Little League teams that Chuchi formed. The storefront was funded in part by state grants approved annually by a committee chaired by a successful lawyer, state senator Gabriel Rivera, D-San Bernardino.

The family gathered quietly at the appointed site. They watched as Soledad laid the wreath at the wall where the names of California's Vietnam war dead were listed. She ran her finger over the name, bowed her head, and walked back to her family. And then each, in turn, approached the wall and traced the name:

Staff Sergeant Benny Sánchez, U.S. Army, Barstow.

Ricardo Pimentel was born in San Bernardino, California, to undocumented Mexican immigrants. His parents valued education and passed on their respect for learning to their children. Ricardo knew early on that he wanted to write. He became a U.S. Navy journalist and has worked as a newspaper reporter and editor in California, Washington, D.C., and Arizona. Currently he is executive editor at the *San Bernardino County Sun.*